Was it all in her imagination?

Jenny had almost dozed off when she heard an odd scraping sound. She sat up, completely awake now, and felt the presence of someone nearby. But there was no one in her room. She remained quiet, listening intently, trying to identify the direction of the sound.

With a sense of shock she realized that the noise came from the virgin's bedroom. But the room was locked—and no one ever used it!

Jenny swung her legs over the side of the bed, hardly daring to breathe. Her mouth was dry and her forehead was damp. Now everything was silent. She must have been dreaming....

ISLAND OF MYSTERY

MARGARET M. SCARIANO

Harlequin Books

TORONTO • NEW YORK • LONDON
AMSTERDAM • PARIS • SYDNEY • HAMBURG
STOCKHOLM • ATHENS • TOKYO • MILAN

Published March 1987
ISBN 0-373-32015-9

Printed in Canada

CHAPTER ONE

FROM THE MOMENT the speedboat left the Risco dock Jenny felt disoriented, as if Monday, June 17, had already disappeared with the rest of civilization's trappings. The bow of the boat rode high, cutting the lake water and sending sprays of icy mist into her face. The water curled away just inches below the rim of the boat. With morbid fascination she stared into the lake, hypnotized by its darkness, a blue so deep it looked almost black—forbidding. Lone Lake, Jenny thought, was the color of infinity. The isolated surroundings brought a chill of uneasiness. She wanted to turn back. But to what?

She needed this secretarial position at Lone Lake Island to pay for her graduate studies at the university and she needed the research available at Lone Lake Lodge. As her professor had said, "You need facts, Jenny Fletcher, not romantic notions. Helping Mrs. Hamilton sort and file her family papers for presentation to the Montana Historical Society will give you these facts for your thesis."

Granted, she thought, money and research weren't the only reasons she found herself in the middle of the lake with a seemingly hostile Indian as pilot. Keith

Taylor's persistence in wanting her to marry him had been the deciding factor. He just wouldn't hear no, and continued to burden her with invitations, flowers and gifts. She'd refused to date him, delivered the flowers to the hospital and returned his gifts. But in spite of her saying no, thank you, until her tongue was tired, he hadn't listened. Rooming and boarding at Keith's parents had become impossible, and she hoped this job would prove for Keith the old adage Out of sight, out of mind.

There was a sudden thud to the boat as it cut across the waves. Startled, Jenny glanced down at the churning, angry water. A chill snaked down her spine. She forced herself to look away from the dark water and search out the island that was to be her home for the next few months, thanks to her infinite streak of stubbornness.

"Stubbornness," she said aloud, the word muffled by the noise of the motor. She recalled the carefree days when stubbornness had been a comment on her sixth grade report card, not a trait that had sent her eighty miles by bus, three miles by Jeep and now twenty-five miles by boat. Her father had said that stubbornness was good if it was directed through sound methods toward worthy goals. She did have worthy goals—to complete her master's thesis, to be self-supporting and, equally important, to escape from Keith's pressure.

The boat was heading west now and the late afternoon sun shone on the water, the light reflected by the shimmering waves almost blinding her. The slapping of the water against the boat pounded in rhythmic jolts. She thought back to her one telephone conversation with Mrs. Hamilton confirming this job. "My dear," the woman had said, "it will be a golden opportunity, don't you know, to have at your disposal these historical documents." Jenny knew the personal interviews with Mrs. Hamilton and access to her papers should prove invaluable, as the woman was a granddaughter of Horst Clayborn, who had been heavily involved in Montana water rights, land and politics. Jenny's professor also had told her that Clayborn had been a land pirate in 1900 and that much of the wealth Mrs. Hamilton and her family now enjoyed was a direct result of the man's ruthlessness.

Jenny could imagine the mess the personal papers must be in just by Mrs. Hamilton's flighty conversation. She had skipped from one subject to the next, bridging the changing topics with the phrase "don't you know." When Jenny hung up the phone, she knew she was hired, knew Mrs. Hamilton lived on the island year-round with her two nephews, whom she had reared, and that a "Bobby" would meet her at the bus station in the small town of Risco and bring her by boat to Lone Lake Island.

When the bus had finally rattled into the Risco station, she had peered through the window, trying to guess which young man on the platform was waiting for her. When an Indian in his late twenties had stepped forward, she had been delighted; not because he was Indian, but because Mrs. Hamilton hadn't thought it necessary to explain.

"Good afternoon, Miss Fletcher?" He spoke softly, but his dark eyes bore down at her.

"Yes. Are you . . . Bobby?"

"My name is Bobby Black Bear. Sometimes Mrs. Hamilton shortens it. If you give me your luggage claims, I'll get your bags." He pointed to a topless vehicle at the curb. "You can wait in the Jeep."

Driving the three miles from the Risco station to the boat dock was an experience of a hot wind blowing no good. Her long red hair tangled in the hot breeze and she could almost feel her freckles grow larger in the warm sun. Over the noise of the motor she shouted, "Do you live on the island?"

"Yes." Bobby Black Bear's eyes never left the bumpy, dirt road.

"At the lodge?"

"No." He braked for a stop before crossing the highway and headed down the hillside road toward the lake and the dock.

"Just you and Mrs. Hamilton and her two nephews live on that island, then?"

"No. Mrs. Hamilton has Lone Willow, who does the light housework and doubles as a companion. There's usually a cook. And once a month a man and his wife come from Risco to do the heavy cleaning—windows and waxing floors. And—" Bobby Black Bear glanced quickly at her, his dark eyes hooded "—secretaries." His lips thinned as he added, "Mrs. Hamilton has had other secretaries before you." He turned on the car radio.

What did he mean, "other secretaries"? Was Mrs. Hamilton difficult to work for? Or perhaps the isolation got to them—cut off from the main land.... Jenny remembered Lawyer Williams's remark when she'd told him she was taking this job. "Grace Hamilton's a fine woman," he'd said, "but I owe it to you to warn you that that island she lives on ... well, let's just say it's different. Some people can't handle it."

Was that the reason for the turnover in secretaries? The isolation? Why, then, did she suddenly feel uneasy—as if she were on the threshold of a turning point in her life from which there could be no return. The utter contempt in Bobby Black Bear's voice when he mentioned secretaries did not bode well for the future. Her mouth was dry and her heart pounded. She tried to think of other, more rational reasons for the turnover. Maybe the job was too demanding. Or maybe it was just plain boring. What was she getting herself into?

She leaned over and switched off the radio. "Hey, Bobby Black Bear, how come the other secretaries didn't stay?"

He glanced quickly at her and then back to the dirt road. His mouth tightened. "They were not honorable, took advantage of the situation." His voice was hard, angry sounding.

"And you think that because I'm a secretary, I'm like the others, not honorable?" she demanded, suddenly angry herself.

"I didn't say that, Miss Fletcher."

"'Jenny,'" she snapped. Leaning forward, she turned in her seat to look at him. "Listen, Bobby Black Bear, I didn't prejudge you and it's not fair for you to do it to me. Give me a chance, at least."

Bobby Black Bear kept his eyes on the road and appeared not to hear. Finally he grumbled, "Fair enough, Miss...ah, Jenny." Turning into a parking lot by the lakefront, he parked the Jeep and turned to face her. "A little advice, though. Don't take sides."

His voice held a warning note that sent a shiver down her spine. *Sides to what,* she wondered, but before she could ask, he was out of the Jeep and heading for the boat. Almost unwillingly, she followed him. She had been thrilled to get this job and had looked forward to a productive summer. Suddenly she wasn't so sure. If everyone on the island were as surly and mysterious as Bobby Black Bear, it was certainly going to be a lonely couple of months.

Settling her in the boat, he pushed it away from the dock and jumped lightly in.

"What did you mean, 'taking sides'?" she asked, as the boat drifted lifelessly in the dark waters.

He shrugged, fiddling with various knobs and levers, then finally replied, "Just enjoy your job—while it lasts."

He certainly wasn't a representative of Welcome Wagon, she thought, but she was determined not to let him scare her off. Reaching into her purse, she pulled out her scarf and tied it around her head. "It will," she declared firmly. "I'll make that job last!"

Bobby Black Bear looked surprised at her outburst, but merely asked, "You're ready, then?"

"How long will it take us?"

"A little over an hour. We leave this bay and pass between those two small islands—they're called 'the narrows.' Then we're in the main part of the lake where it's rougher and slower. Lone Lake Lodge is almost at the end of the lake." He pressed the starter and they headed out.

As the dock and cars in the parking lot grew smaller, her apprehension and doubts grew larger.

It wasn't as if she were opposed to helpful advice. That was probably what she missed most—her parents' counseling and concern. Two years ago this past February her safe, loving world had crumbled. Her parents, coming home from a football game, had been killed instantly in a car wreck.

Her father had owned the hardware store in Elrod, Illinois, a town of five thousand people, south of Chicago. Her family had been a close one; partly because her parents were older when she was born and partly because they weren't struggling to establish themselves financially or socially. And they were close because they only had one another—except for Aunt Blanche, her father's elder sister.

After the tragic accident, Jenny had applied for the National Exchange Student Program for her senior year and was accepted at Montana University in Missoula. Because history graduates had limited job opportunities, she decided to get her master's and qualify for college teaching. The insurance money would not cover the additional education, so this summer job was essential both financially and scholastically. There was no way she could go back to Illinois yet—even to see Aunt Blanche.

A picture of her aunt flashed through her mind. *What a love she is,* Jenny thought. She remembered the day she'd told Aunt Blanche about attending school in Missoula. The old woman hadn't said a word, but had gone to her cedar hope chest and taken out a bundle of letters. "Thought Missoula sounded familiar, Jenny," she'd said, settling herself in a sagging armchair. "That's where my old beau Wilbur Williams was from. Met him when we attended Northwestern U. He wanted to marry me, but he was so…legal and regimented." She studied the letters for a moment and then looked up. "To tell you the truth, Jenny, he bored me. And, my dear, you can forgive a man for anything except boredom."

Aunt Blanche had written Wilbur Williams, and a few days after Jenny arrived in Missoula, she called on him. He arranged for her to room and board with Mr. and Mrs. Taylor, and thus she met their son, Keith. It was a shame, she thought, that she could not care for Keith. It would be nice to have someone in this world, the way her parents had had each other. They had married after a three-day whirlwind courtship. "Instant love," her mother used to say, smiling at her father. "With real, lasting flavor" Dad always added tenderly.

Jenny shifted around on her seat. It seemed the monotonous sound of the motor and the endless body of water would go on forever. When they passed between the narrows, the size of the main part of the lake overwhelmed her. The water had an angry gray look and the waves knocked threateningly on the bottom of the boat. The snow-frosted mountain peaks of Glacier Park range enclosed the lake like barriers shutting out the real world. The trees stole down to the water's edge, their foliage hiding any cozy lakefront homes. Now and then a gray dock, like a dismembered arm, extended out from the beach. Jenny felt as if the world were closing in on her, and there was no escaping now. It wasn't as though she could simply walk down to the corner, catch a bus and leave if she didn't like what awaited her. A sudden, unexplainable cold fear shivered inside her. She was trapped.

Now she could see the island, a dark mass dense with trees. Steep cliffs like a fortress met the crashing waves. The boat swerved and she gripped the side, glancing back at Bobby Black Bear. He cut the engine and pointed down into the water. As the boat gradually slowed, she looked over the side. She could see the bottom of the lake now. And what a view! Like the remnants of an ancient civilization, gigantic boulders covered the floor of the lake. The boat glided quietly over the huge rocks toward the dock in a silence as ominous as the miniature Atlantis below the water.

"How deep is it here?" she asked.

"Thirty to forty feet." Bobby Black Bear stood up and moved to the bow as the boat drifted closer to the dock. Grabbing the rope, he stood poised, ready to leap to the dock and secure the boat.

She remained seated and looked at the dock extending out from the narrow rocky beach hedged in by the jagged cliffs. She half expected a LaBrea Pits type of deposit showing the skeletal remains of a saber-toothed tiger or giant sloth, or at least hieroglyphics sketched by a primitive people on the cliff walls. The dock was bleached and bare and rested on pilings anchored on the boulders below. No one was on hand to greet them. She felt as if she and Bobby Black Bear were the lone survivors of civilization. She could see no sign of the lodge through the dense stand of pine and spruce.

Bobby Black Bear tied up. "Give me your hand," he ordered, leaning over. "Put your foot on the seat, then step up."

She reached down for her purse on the floor of the boat and stood up. The boat rocked, and she gasped. The last thing she wanted was to topple into that dark water. Bobby Black Bear grabbed her hand firmly, steadying her as she stepped on the seat and then onto the dock. Waiting while he climbed back into the boat for her luggage, she again looked down into the water. The huge, square boulders fascinated her. Had they broken away from the cliffs centuries ago? Or were pieces of the island still being eroded, joining those already lying on the bottom?

Bobby Black Bear, luggage in hand, stepped adeptly onto the deck. Suddenly a shadow, long and black, darted among the rocks underwater. She jumped back from the edge of the dock, her voice almost paralyzed by fear. She grabbed at Bobby Black Bear's shirt, then pointed into the lake. "There's something down there, something dark in the water," she croaked.

Bobby Black Bear shrugged. He set her luggage down and looked into the water. "Probably a dead-head. They're a real hazard."

When she didn't comment, he added. "A water-soaked log, you know."

She nodded and, leaning over, looked again into the water. Nothing. Not a bubble or a ripple. Nothing but the silent gray boulders.

Mentally shrugging off her fear, she followed Bobby Black Bear along the narrow dock. As they neared the end of the pier, she saw a slit in the trees and a path leading into the forest. *Must lead to the house,* she thought. She'd be glad to get there and off this dock. She kept glancing back at the boat, as though she might see someone there. But who? There was no one on the dock but Bobby Black Bear and her.

Bobby Black Bear was almost to the graveled path leading up through the trees. Suddenly there was the sound of thrashing water alongside her and she caught a glimpse of something black slithering under the sur-face. She started running. The water thrashed again, and just as she caught up with Bobby Black Bear, someone called. "Hey, wait. You must be the new secretary. Welcome to Lone Lake Island."

She stopped, but couldn't turn around, her legs would not cooperate.

Bobby Black Bear also stopped at the sound of the voice. Setting the luggage down, he pushed past her.

"Glenn!" He called out. "When did you get back? Good to see you."

Pulling herself together, she turned to see Bobby Black Bear hurrying toward a man in a black wet suit sitting on the dock, his finned feet dangling above the water. She went limp with relief. Her mind hadn't been tricking her; she really had seen something. Then she was angry, as much at herself for her irrational fear as at the man playing hide and seek and scaring her. How humiliating to be caught shying on the dock like some nervous colt!

Bobby Black Bear's face was far from inscrutable now. He wore a wide smile as he punched playfully at the man's upper arm. It was as though this black-suited man had pressed a button releasing the Indian's alter ego. The obvious pleasure of their reunion softened the anger within her.

She walked toward the two men. Now that the swimmer had removed his mask, she could see he was as dark haired as Bobby Black Bear, but his hair was a mass of curls.

"Jenny, Glenn Larabie." Bobby Black Bear crouched beside his friend. "One of Mrs. Hamilton's infamous nephews."

She couldn't help smiling as Glenn flipped his flippers onto the dock and awkwardly stood up, tall and lean. "Jenny—" Glenn nodded his acknowledgment.

Some deadhead, Jenny thought. "You startled me. I was thinking about lost civilizations and prehistoric monsters and suddenly there was a black creature slithering among those—" She stopped, embarrassed by her almost hysterical rambling. She looked up at Glenn, expecting to see a smile of welcome or even a look of amusement on his face. But his expression was like a mask. Only his eyes, dark pools of ice water, reflected his feelings. No wonder they couldn't keep secretaries on this island, she thought. The two men she'd met were nothing short of hostile. If she could walk on water, she'd take off for Risco right now.

With as much dignity as she could muster, she turned and walked stiffly toward the path.

"Nice to meet you, new secretary," Glenn called out, adding, "maybe you'd better wait for Bobby Black Bear. It's pretty dark going through the trees—even for your jade-green eyes."

Jenny stopped. She had to admit, she didn't really want to plunge into the forest by herself. "I'll wait," she said. "I just didn't want to intrude."

"Well, that's a first—at least for the secretaries I've known," Glenn said, his tone suddenly angry. He and Bobby Black Bear joined her at the end of the dock.

"How was your trip, Glenn?" asked the Indian.

"Successful, BB." Like a chameleon Glenn's attitude changed swiftly in response to a new situation. Draping his arm on Bobby Black Bear's shoulder, he added. "Got the financial backing all lined up. California money. But—" his expression sobered "—the tough job is ahead of me. I've got to convince Aunt Grace that development of the island would be more ecologically sound, not to mention financially advantageous, than her leaving it to the state for some littered, cramped, public campground. An island tent city.''

What an angry man, Jenny thought. He was like a volcano, one minute quiet and the next minute erupting.

''Well, you're going to have to do some selling job, Glenn. Your Aunt Grace is uptight about retribution. She wears her guilt like war paint.'' Bobby Black Bear shook his head.

Glenn nodded but said nothing.

''Guilt?'' Jenny murmured.

''Yes, guilt!'' Glenn suddenly blazed, his fists clenched. Then almost visibly he restrained himself, lowering his voice and relaxing his hands. ''Something my dear brother, Martin, feeds in large doses to Aunt Grace, hoping he can get the island for himself.'' He spoke quietly, but Jenny felt the tension behind them like the pressure preceding a violent storm. She said nothing, almost afraid that any sound would unleash the obvious fury raging within him.

''Martin, Glenn's elder brother, Jenny, is really big on conservation,'' explained Bobby Black Bear. ''He wants to preserve the island in its natural state, status quo, so to speak.''

''Nothing remains unchanged. That's against the laws of nature,'' Glenn snapped. ''But nature boy Martin can't see that, any more than he can see how it takes money to maintain this island. My plans are both ecologically and financially sound, with controlled housing development, recreational sites for public beaches and a marina. No camping, but cottages to rent.''

''Hey, man, I'd better get Jenny up to the house, or your Aunt Grace will have my scalp—figuratively speaking, of course!''

''You'll get used to BB's little ethnic jokes, Jenny,'' said Glenn with a mocking smile. ''He likes to play Indian.''

''I am Indian.'' Bobby Black Bear's voice echoed the heritage of a proud, young chieftain leading his people. Obviously Glenn and Bobby Black Bear were good friends. Although they joked and teased, they respected each other.

Glenn clapped him on the back. ''And a good one. Guess I have time for a couple more dives.''

Jenny couldn't help but notice the ripple of muscles along Glenn's athletic frame as he flip-flopped toward the edge of the dock. But what a volatile man! His moods rolled up and down like a yo-yo.

Turning, he said, ''See you later, Jenny New Secretary, BB.''

She nodded and, glancing up at him, tried an impersonal, secretarial smile, then glanced away, surprised by his look of vulnerability. Why he was just as uneasy as she!

CHAPTER TWO

SILENTLY BOBBY BLACK BEAR led the way up the winding path. Although they had only walked ten or twelve yards, Jenny could no longer see the lake. Ahead the path climbed higher and higher. The dark, dense forest closed around them. Like a primeval forest, she thought, and quickened her steps to stay closer to her guide. The shadowed path was almost vertical now. She tried to concentrate on her footing rather than let her thoughts stray to worries of job security, the hostility of the two men, the eerie ambience of the island. Twice she stumbled over exposed roots on the path as she glanced into the woods—so dark, so forbidding.

They must have walked ten minutes, when suddenly the path veered sharply to the left. There upon the cliffs stood the house. From the pathway Jenny saw how the trees hid the view of the house from the dock. Since they had approached the island from the opposite direction, the house had not been visible from the boat. But what inappropriate architecture for a lake home! It was Victorian-style with pointed-arch windows, at least on the main floor. The second, third and fourth stories had narrow, stingy windows of rectangular shape. An old iron fire-escape ladder scaled the house to the top floor. A wide veranda extended halfway around the house, and dark-stained wicker chairs, couches and tables were scattered about.

"What a huge house!" she exclaimed. "How many rooms?"

Bobby Black Bear counted off on his fingers. "There are seven bedrooms, four-and-a-half bathrooms, a living room, library, kitchen and dining room, and a ballroom on the fourth floor. That doesn't count the cellar."

"Ballroom? And seven bedrooms?"

"Seven," he said, then added quietly, "if you don't count the virgin's bedroom. That would make eight."

"Virgin's bedroom?" Jenny echoed in disbelief. But his expression was serious.

"When old man Clayborn built this house around 1890, he had one son, Sheldon Clayborn, and two daughters, Amy and Abigail." Bobby Black Bear sounded like a guide lecturing to a tourist. His tone was a boring monotone. "In those days it was customary to protect a daughter's virginity. So many houses in England and Spain, and in America, too, were built with a bedroom off the parents' bedroom—the only entrance to this room being through the parents' room. Since his daughters were grown and his son, Sheldon, was courting, Clayborn took the second floor for his sleeping quarters and turned the third floor, complete with virgin's bedroom, over to Sheldon for when he married."

Jenny nodded, her mind visualizing a Victorian, night-capped father snoozing with one eye open and focused on the door to his daughter's room, ever vigilant for her virginity. But she had little time to continue her daydream, for Bobby Black Bear had started up the wide steps to the veranda. She followed, stopping frequently to look back over her shoulder at her surroundings. There were no trees or shrubs around the house—perhaps they wouldn't grow in the rocky soil. The lake, far below, pounded against the cliffs, retreated in foam and gathering force, pounded again. Birds dotted the sky, swooping down to the lake in death dives for food, their eerie cries the only alleviation to the brooding silence.

Except for the birds there was no sign of life. Again she had that eerie feeling she'd felt when she'd looked into the lake at the piles of boulders—a civilization gone. Now this house seemed to be of another era, too—almost as though it were dead and waiting to slide into the lake.

Bobby Black Bear must have noticed her looking back at the rocky ledge and the lake below. "Jenny, stay off that point," he warned. "Stick to the paths. Periodically chunks of the cliff crash into the lake." He opened one of the double doors and stepped aside for her to enter. "One of Clayborn's daughters—I think it was Amy—fell to her death from that point. A piece of rock just gave way...."

Jenny shuddered and stepped gingerly into a long, narrow hallway. A staircase to her left curved up to the floor above and four doors led off from the hall.

Setting her luggage at the foot of the stairs, Bobby Black Bear called out, "Ruthie. Oh, Ruthie."

The door at the end of the hall on the left opened and Jenny heard a clacking sound before she saw anyone or anything. Then a slender girl stepped into the hall and walked toward them. Her black hair hung in braids, and as she came closer, Jenny saw the double-stranded necklace of porcupine quills that encircled her golden brown neck and hung almost to her waist. As she walked, the necklace swayed and the quills made a soft clacking sound, like dried seeds in a pod. The quills, placed closely together, were fastened to rawhide. Although such necklaces were supposedly common to the Indian culture, this was the first one Jenny had seen outside a museum.

"She's lovely! Your sister?" Jenny asked quietly.

"I know all Indians look alike," Bobby Black Bear said, "but Ruthie is no relation. Same tribe, but no relation."

Ruthie glided down the hall. When she reached them, she didn't even glance at Bobby Black Bear. "Good afternoon, Miss Fletcher." Her voice was soft and lilting. "I am Lone Willow." She looked at Bobby Black Bear then and seemed to raise her head defiantly.

Bobby Black Bear grinned and then with mock seriousness bowed. "Forgive me, Lone Willow. Indian Brave forget maiden's Indian name." For some reason his mocking ways reminded Jenny of Glenn Larabie's manner. He straightened and, turning to Jenny, said, "Lone Willow is active in the Indian cause."

"You may take Miss Fletcher's luggage to the third floor, Bobby Black Bear. Mrs. Hamilton has assigned her the parents' room."

"Is that the room that adjoins the, a . . . a virgin's bedroom?" Jenny asked.

"Yes," Lone Willow answered, closing the front door and stepping aside for Bobby Black Bear to lead the way. "But the door between is kept locked—ever since Miss Merci died."

Bobby Black Bear tossed words of explanation over his shoulder as he climbed the stairs. "Miss Merci was Grace Hamilton's sister, quite a bit younger than Mrs. Hamilton. Ten or twelve years, I believe. Miss Merci was the mother of Glenn and Martin. Her husband deserted her. Later she drowned in a boating accident. Mrs. Hamilton raised her boys."

Lone Willow followed Bobby Black Bear, and Jenny brought up the rear. "Does Mrs. Hamilton know I have arrived? Perhaps we should let her know in case she wants me to start in right away."

"She knows," Lone Willow said, never breaking her stride. "She saw you through her spyglass as you docked."

"I didn't think you could see the dock from the house," Jenny said.

"From Mrs. Hamilton's wing the dock is visible. Her room has windows on three sides—two in her bedroom and one in the bathroom. She has a wide view of the dock and the lake."

No wonder she'd felt as if someone were watching her, Jenny thought. Glenn, slithering about among the rocks in his wet suit, had only increased her uneasiness.

They had reached the second floor, and the stairs leading up to the next floor were curved and steeper.

"Mrs. Hamilton's room is there." Lone Willow pointed to a doorway. "These two bedrooms with the bath between belong to Glenn and Martin."

They finally reached the third floor, and Jenny decided right then that her memory had better be good or she'd be worn out in a week, climbing the stairs for things she'd forgotten. The trick to survival in this house, Jenny figured, must be to pack a bag for all the things needed during the day—sweater, lipstick, comb, Kleenex—and then park it on the first flight of steps.

"This is where I sleep." Lone Willow pointed to a corner bedroom. "And you are diagonally across from me."

"Who uses this room?" Jenny looked into the room next to Lone Willow's.

"No one. It is very small. Mrs. Hamilton thought you would be more comfortable in the parents' bedroom." She opened the door and they entered a large room.

Bobby Black Bear set the luggage down, placing one suitcase on the luggage rack at the foot of the bed. "I'll leave you girls now. You're in good hands, Jenny. See you later, Ru—Lone Willow."

"Bye. Thanks," said Jenny as he left the room.

"Oh, Bobby Black Bear," Lone Willow called out, hurrying to the doorway, "Mrs. Hamilton would like you to join us for dinner tonight. Cocktails at six in the library. See you then." And Jenny heard Bobby Black Bear hurrying down the stairs.

Lone Willow led the way across the room, patting a pillow, straightening a lampshade, smoothing the bedspread. It was furnished as a sitting room as well as a bedroom. It was a lovely room, thought Jenny, but in a museum-cold way. The walls were papered in a green-and-white stripe and the drapes were brocade of the same green, looped back with a tasseled cord. A patterned glass curtain hung behind the drape, filtering the light. An ornately carved, black walnut bed with, on one side, a flower stand serving as a bedside table and, on the other, a bureau with wooden carved grape-and-leaf drawer pulls took up one-third of the room. Two matching pale mauve, tufted satin chairs were placed by the front window with a small, marble-topped table between them. There was a petite writing desk on which was placed a Jane Eyre brass candle holder with a green candle. The door leading into the virgin's bedroom was on the same wall as a black marble fireplace.

"Here's the closet to hang your clothes, and the bureau is empty, Miss Fletcher." Lone Willow opened the bathroom door and leaned in, apparently checking to see if all was in order. "Would you like me to unpack for you?"

"Do call me 'Jenny.' I feel like you're talking to someone else when you say 'Miss Fletcher.' And no, thanks, I'm used to doing for myself. Why don't you sit down and keep me company while I unpack?"

Lone Willow shook her head. "Mrs. Hamilton will expect me to tell her that you are getting settled in." She headed for the door. "Dinner is at six-thirty. Mrs. Hamilton invites you to join her and her nephews in the library at six for cocktails."

"Is it formal?" Jenny had packed for vacation living, shorts and slacks with a few skirts and blouses and sweaters for secretarial duties.

"Oh, no. Not formal—just 'civilized, don't you know'—as Mrs. Hamilton puts it." Lone Willow's dark eyes twinkled briefly and then the stoic, expressionless look returned. She hesitated at the doorway. "And Jenny, that door to the virgin's bedroom is always kept locked. Think nothing of it. Mrs. Hamilton's sister used it as a study when she lived here with her family. Her things are still in there."

"I understand." Jenny smiled at her, hoping to see the mask lift and her eyes brighten again, but Lone Willow's face remained impassive.

The door closed and Jenny was alone. Suddenly she was tired. She glanced at her watch. Four-thirty. She'd unpack and hang up her clothes and then have a quick bath. Perhaps she'd lie down for a few minutes before dressing. It had been a long day.

She lay on the bed, eyes closed, completely relaxed after the soothing bath. It seemed ages since she had left Missoula and Keith. She said the name Keith aloud, but felt no longing. Keith had said, "Absence makes the heart grow fonder."

His impassioned words came back. "Don't say no outright. Think about it, Jenny. I know I can make you happy." She wished she could have made him realize she wasn't interested in marriage, only friendship. Unexpectedly her thoughts leaped to Glenn. Which was the true Glenn? The handsome, confident man who talked enthusiastically with Bobby Black Bear about his plans for the island, or the angry, sarcastic intense one who had greeted her on the dock? Almost a dual personality, she thought; a man who could break a heart with one cold look, or set it in perpetual motion with a single smile.

Warm, she pushed the afghan aside. Well, she thought, she certainly had her work cut out for her. She had to be the perfect secretary for Mrs. Hamilton to prove to Glenn and Bobby Black Bear that all secretaries were not alike.

Her thoughts drifted to Lone Willow. A strange young woman, she thought, seemingly emotionless, and with such a soft voice. She didn't seem like the militant type at all. But perhaps her reticence, too, could be attributed to the general dislike of secretaries that seemed to pervade the island.

Jenny had almost dozed off, when she heard a strange, scraping sound. Startled, she sat up. Completely awake now, she sensed the presence of someone nearby, but there was no one in her room. She sat still, listening intently, trying to identify the direction of the sound. It was with a sense of shock that she realized it came from the virgin's bedroom. But it couldn't, she thought. The room was locked! No one ever used it. With heart pounding, she swung her legs over the side of the bed and sat on the edge. Hardly daring to breathe, she strained to listen. Her mouth was dry and her forehead wet. But now all she heard was a clacking sound—like seeds in a pod. The bed creaked as she stood up. Silence now. Slowly she exhaled. She must have been dreaming.

CHAPTER THREE

THERE WAS NO NEED to be nervous, Jenny told herself firmly, standing before the library door. Mrs. Hamilton, she was sure, was a fine lady. She was overreacting, and all because of a strange noise she thought she heard from a supposedly locked room in broad daylight. Ridiculous! Nevertheless a shiver ran up her spine, and she wiped her damp palms on her skirt as the clacking sound replayed in her mind.

Enough, she told herself sternly. For the umpteenth time she smoothed her sweater over the denim skirt, flipped her hair loose from the collar and, finally taking a deep breath, knocked. It was five-thirty, a few minutes early, but better early than late, surely.

"Door's open. Come in," a voice, easy and relaxed sounding, called out.

Opening the door, she stepped inside the library. A fire glowed in the rock fireplace and on either side of it bookshelves lined the wall. A man slouched in a love seat, his long legs stretched out in front of the fire.

He stood, unfolding his long frame with a fluid, almost liquid motion. "Hello. I'm Martin Larabie, Glenn's brother. I know you've met him. He manages to meet all the pretty girls first. And you must be

Aunt Grace's *latest* secretary.'' With a flowing motion of his hand, he indicated that she should sit.

At the emphasis on "latest," Jenny's mouth tightened as she tilted her chin up defiantly. She wanted to say, "Not the latest secretary, but the last," but instead answered demurely, "Yes, I'm here for the summer to help your aunt organize family papers. I'm Jenny Fletcher.'' She sat down on the love seat.

He stood in front of her, looking down. He was tall like his brother, Glenn, but there the resemblance ended. Martin was blond and his build was slighter, more hungry-looking than Glenn's lean, muscular frame.

She looked around the room. Directly across from the green chintz-covered love seat were two yellow chairs with a maple table between them. On the opposite wall of the fireplace was an executive desk with a typewriter on it. The two-drawer file cabinet was placed so it could be reached without rising from the desk chair. Three stacks of boxes, each filled with four cartons, lined the wall next to the file. An oversize tea cart with its leaves extended was on the other side of the desk. Obviously it served as a portable bar, as it held several bottles and a decanter, glasses and a silver ice bucket.

She glanced up at Martin. He smiled as though he were amused with her scrutiny of the room. Half bowing, he nodded toward the love seat. "May I?"

Such a courtly man, she thought, almost old-fashioned. What a contrast from his brother! She wanted to respond in the same gracious style, but was at a loss to do more than extend her hand toward the other half of the love seat.

Martin sat down, turning slightly to face her. "One thing about Aunt Grace, Jenny," he said, smiling, "she follows a rigid time schedule. Weren't you told six in the library?"

"Yes, but...I thought it better to be early than late, and particularly on my first meeting with Mrs. Hamilton." She knew she was sputtering like a guilty schoolgirl. Why did she feel so defensive? So what if there had been secretaries before her?

"Your first lesson in 'Aunt Graceism' is BE PUNCTUAL." Martin's smile negated any sarcastic tone. "Not too early and never late. As scatter-brained as Aunt Grace might seem, don't you believe it. She's excitable, flighty, but she's also smart—even shrewd. Sticking to a time schedule for cocktails, breakfast, lunch, dinner, rising and retiring gives her some hold on the reality of time. And she knows that her time is...ah, limited."

"Oh?" queried Jenny. "But I thought Mrs. Hamilton was in her early sixties. That's not old. Isn't she well?" She hoped she wouldn't be spending her time baby-sitting a sick woman rather than gathering historical research.

Martin threw back his head and laughed. "Aunt Grace well? She's fairly blooming with health! She's a health addict! She eats berries and nuts and natural cereals. She's special." His voice vibrated with devotion. "She even has Bobby Black Bear farming an organic garden for her down on Shadow Cove."

"Shadow Cove?" Jenny queried.

"That's where Bobby Black Bear lives—about a mile and a half from here. It's the only piece of land on this island that doesn't belong to Aunt Grace. Bobby Black Bear, as his father was, is in the lumber business. Has a degree in forestry. He owns a mill in Risco. Most of his time is spent in obtaining leases and scouting out timber."

Martin stood up and began to pace in front of her. "Grandfather Clayborn deeded ten acres to Bobby Black Bear's grandfather for some reason or other."

"And Bobby Black Bear lives there by himself?" Jenny asked.

"Yes, his grandmother reared him. She died some months ago. His father, George Lightfoot, died in the boating accident with my mother."

"How tragic!" She felt the familiar hurt deep inside. Would she ever be able to speak as matter-of-factly of her parents as Martin did of his mother?

"Never did find the boat. Guess it's at the bottom of the lake someplace. Glenn and I were very young. Aunt Grace reared us as her own." Martin sat down on the love seat again.

"Do you live here all year long, then?" Jenny asked.

"Yes, I'm a teacher at Risco Junior College—teach sociology. I commute by boat."

"And your brother has something to do with land—he's not a teacher like you."

Martin smiled and shook his head. "Glenn couldn't stand the routine of teaching. He's the restless type.

Works for a national land development company and flies all over the country, making deals. In between developments he lives on the island.

"But enough of this," he continued, half turning to face her. "How about you? Aunt Grace says you're working on your master's. You don't look old enough to be in graduate school." His voice was low and his manner interested and gracious.

"I'm twenty-four," Jenny said defensively, and could have kicked herself. Why couldn't she have just smiled in a sophisticated and cool way?

Martin nodded. "Well, you're old enough to know what you want. But why isolate yourself at Lone Lake Lodge? Someone like you must have lots of job offers, to say nothing of boyfriends."

He was out to charm her, Jenny thought, and doing a good job of it. This time she simply answered him with a smile. But Martin wasn't about to settle for a wordless smile for an answer.

"Well?" he queried. "Why did you want to isolate yourself here for the summer?" There was a demanding note in his voice that reminded her of Glenn's arrogant manner, but his manner was less offensive.

"It's twofold," she told him. "I need the money to finish my education and I need the research."

"That's right. Aunt Grace did say you were a history major. So you're actually interested in that mess of papers of hers?" His joking tone suggested he found the idea amusing. Was she perhaps putting too much faith in the historical value of Mrs. Hamilton's papers?

"I'm hoping to find them useful," she said primly. "I've completed the course work and just have my thesis left."

Martin threw back his head and laughed. "Just your thesis! You are an optimist. That's a large part of the master's program, isn't it?"

"It is an important part," she conceded, "but I have the outline approved and much of the research done." What was it about this man that forced her to explain things?

"What's your theme, or whatever it's called?" Martin asked.

"That the development of the West was influenced by the type of people who settled it—the malcontents of the East, whatever their trade or profession." She answered almost by rote. It had been difficult for her to state concisely her intentions and her professor had been adamant in demanding a statement of purpose backed by facts, not romantic theories.

"Well, you should be able to get lots of material from Aunt Grace if you can sort out the mess. She has papers and documents dating back beyond the turn of the century." Martin stood abruptly and walked toward the fireplace. He poked the smoldering log and it burst into flame again. He laid another log on the grate, muttering something she couldn't catch.

"I beg your pardon—I didn't hear you." Leaning forward on the love seat, she was surprised to see that he held the fire poker as if it were a weapon, his knuckles white with clenching.

Abruptly replacing the poker in the stand, he turned around, his expression solemn. "I said, Jenny, I need your help."

Her help? She wanted to laugh. This confident, courtly man asking for her help? And she'd only been on the island a few hours. But instead she simply asked, "How can I help you?" She figured two could play the charming game. And it was a nice change from the way Glenn had acted.

"With Aunt Grace. Oh, I can tell you will be competent and a big help in organization, Jenny. Aunt Grace said you came highly recommended. But I mean for you to help her more subtly. Guide her. Help her to see that it is her duty to preserve this island wilderness—leave it in its natural state—as a monument to the past. Conserve the beauty of untouched wilderness." His voice trembled. Slowly he walked back to the love seat, his head bowed, and sat down. Taking her hand in his, he looked into her eyes. "This should be easy for you to understand," he continued fervently. "You're a history major and know how important the past is. What better way than a virgin island unmolested by modern civilization?"

She felt her cheeks grow warm. Martin's plea sounded sincere. But this was obviously the "taking sides" issue Bobby Black Bear had warned her about. And perhaps, too, this was why the other secretaries hadn't lasted. No, she decided, she just had to stay neutral between the brothers. Besides, it was none of her business.

The clock struck its first note, startling her. She jerked her hand from Martin's, and at that moment the door opened and a graying blond woman entered. She was about Jenny's height, but with a full, matronly figure.

The clock chimed for the second time. Jenny stood.

"Good evening. I'm Grace Hamilton. You must be Jenny Fletcher." She walked toward Jenny with her hands outstretched. Taking both Jenny's hands in hers, she squeezed them tightly.

"Mrs. Hamilton. I'm happy to meet you and I'm looking forward to working with you this summer."

Mrs. Hamilton's gray-green eyes looked directly into hers.

"Delighted to have you, don't you know," said the woman, releasing her hands. She sat down in one of the chairs opposite the love seat. "Good evening, Martin, dear. I see you and Jenny have met."

"Your secretaries get prettier each time, Aunt Grace." Martin turned to Jenny. "Why don't you sit here?" He pointed to the other yellow chair. When she was seated, he sat on the arm of the chair.

It was almost as if she were watching a time-oriented play, the chiming of the clock being the cue. First Glenn charged through the doorway as if propelled by an unknown force, and then Lone Willow and Bobby Black Bear entered together. The sound of the sixth chime still vibrated.

"I'm glad we're not late, Mrs. Hamilton." Lone Willow knelt beside the woman's chair. "I went down to Bobby Black Bear's to get fresh carrots for your dinner.'' She sounded breathless and had obviously hurried to be on time. Jenny noticed none of the antagonism between her and Bobby Black Bear she'd felt when she'd arrived. Indeed, she could almost feel the warmth between them now.

Lone Willow looked up from her place beside Mrs. Hamilton's chair. ''I gave the carrots to the new cook and asked that he serve them tonight.''

''Thank you, dear. I'm sure Mr. Alger will oblige.'' Mrs. Hamilton twirled a lock of her hair around her index finger. Such a funny habit for one apparently so composed.

''Good evening, Mrs. Hamilton.'' Bobby Black Bear stood in front of her. ''Thank you for inviting me to dinner.''

''Always a pleasure to have you, don't you know.''

''Jenny—'' Bobby Black Bear smiled ''—you look so . . . so natural sitting there.''

Martin threw back his head and laughed. ''Natural? Natural? You make her sound dead!'' He leaned over and took her hand. ''Jenny is very much alive. Like a melody that lingers in my mind.''

''You know that isn't what Bobby Black Bear meant, Martin,'' Glenn snapped. He crossed the room to the tea cart. ''Will you have the usual, Aunt Grace?''

''Yes, Glenn.'' Mrs. Hamilton turned to Jenny. ''I always have a glass of wine before dinner, dear. I find the cocktail hour so offensive, don't you know, but wine, prepared especially for me with no additives, is at least healthy.''

After they had given their cocktail order, Glenn handed a tray to Bobby Black Bear with the wine and drinks on it.

Bobby Black Bear walked stiffly, as though still smarting from Martin's laughter, across the room and handed the wine to Mrs. Hamilton.

"Thank you, Bobby." Mrs. Hamilton held the wine in one hand and with her other patted his arm. "These boys," she bubbled, "well, men, really, are like bear cubs, always teasing each other."

No one said anything. Jenny glanced at Mrs. Hamilton to see if she were aware of the tension permeating the room, but she seemed oblivious to the mood as she sipped her wine and fingered her strand of hair.

Bobby Black Bear, his face immobile, passed the drinks to the rest of them. "I'd like to make a toast." Martin stood.

"Here, here." Glenn tapped a spoon against his glass.

"To the fairer sex—Aunt Grace, Ruthie and Jenny—and their summer's fulfillment." Martin drained his drink.

She'd drink to that. Her summer had to be fulfilled with work. She glanced at Lone Willow, or was it Ruthie? It certainly was confusing. Was she "Ruthie" at the cocktail hour and "Lone Willow" during working hours, or was it only Martin who called her "Ruthie"? Out of the corner of her eye, Jenny glanced at the young woman. She sat tightly erect, her face, as usual, impassive.

A man appeared in the doorway, wearing a white stained butcher apron around his paunchy middle. "Dinner's ready," he announced gruffly. His head was shaved bald. Reddish sideburns running into a goatee filled out his face, and a thick mustache hung over his upper lip.

Mrs. Hamilton stared at him. Edging forward on her chair, she squinted, then shook her head. Holding her wrist at a distance, she studied her watch. "Oh, dear, Mr. Alger, you're early." She leaned forward to look at him, but he half turned, as if to escape her scrutiny. "We always dine at six-thirty, don't you know."

"No, ma'am." He shrugged. "All I know is it's ready. Even them carrots." Now his eyes shifted around the room as though he were appraising not only the furnishings but the people. When his glance reached Jenny, he glared at her as though she had no right to being there. What was it with the men on this island, Jenny mused, first Bobby Black Bear, then Glenn, and now this Mr. Alger all acting as if she were some kind of enemy. A strange and confusing set of relationships all-around, and she wondered how they had all managed to coexist peacefully for so long.

Mrs. Hamilton was rambling on about the necessity of a schedule. Jenny looked around at the others, but nobody seemed to have noticed Mr. Alger's glare. Maybe she was overreacting again. Maybe he glared at everyone. She had no idea, but his look of pure hatred made her decidedly uneasy.

"It's all right, Aunt Grace," Glenn said. "I'll explain the time schedule to you later, Alger." Glenn stood in front of Mrs. Hamilton and, holding out his hand, helped her to her feet. She slipped her arm through his and they led the way to the dining room.

Jenny thought that Martin would probably escort her, since Bobby Black Bear and Lone Willow had come in together, but, no, Martin half bowed before Lone Willow and they followed Mrs. Hamilton and Glenn. Muttering under his breath, Bobby Black Bear led Jenny to the dining room. She felt like the proverbial stone around the neck—unwanted and burdensome.

The dining room was paneled on three sides in a dark, glossy wood. A large walnut harvest table with heavy straight-backed chairs dominated the center of the room and along one wall a narrow sideboard was built in. The wall directly opposite from the sideboard was all glass. The lake seemed closer to the house from this room, even though the view was still first of the craggy cliff and then of the lake below.

Once they were seated, Martin made every effort to include her in the conversation by compliments and questions concerning her career. In fact, he was almost the life of the party, for no one else seemed inclined to make an effort at conversation. Glenn positively glowered as he toyed with the food, his fork pushing the lumpy, mashed potatoes around like a miniature bulldozer.

After a particularly bad joke from Martin, he looked up and his eyes met Jenny's across the table.

For a brief instant, a sardonic smile flicked across his face. Then his lips tightened and his eyes narrowed into cold slits. He turned away, shutting her out as if he'd slammed a door in her face. It was almost as though he felt she was a threat to him, but for the life of her she couldn't figure out why.

Mrs. Hamilton, fluttering her way through dinner, solicitously offered seconds to everyone and began to chat about how healthy organic vegetables were. Apparently she was oblivious to Glenn's smoldering anger and Bobby Black Bear's sullen silence.

Jenny speared a carrot onto the fork and chewed. It might be organically grown, she thought with an inward grimace, but it was tough and flavorless. To add insult to injury, the roast was dry. Well, maybe Mr. Alger wasn't used to the kitchen yet.

"Aunt Grace." Glenn's voice sounded like a thunderclap after Martin's breezy conversation.

"Yes, Glenn?" Mrs. Hamilton dabbed at her mouth with the linen napkin.

"I realize this is his first day with us, but where did you find this . . . this cook . . . this Sam Alger guy?"

"Martin got him through the employment agency. You know," she added thoughtfully, "Mr. Alger reminds me of someone, but who?" She tapped her chin with her finger. Turning to Jenny, she added, "It's difficult to get help on the island, so isolated, don't you know."

"You certainly haven't had trouble getting secretaries." Glenn raised his wineglass in Jenny's direction, but more in a taunt than a toast. "You've had three in the past two months."

Oh, great, Jenny thought. If Mrs. Hamilton continues at that rate, I'll be out of here in two and a half weeks. Then it'll be back to Missoula with no job, no master's research and Keith pressing his case.

"Now, Glenn—" Mrs. Hamilton shook her finger at him "—one secretary had morning sickness, and you know I do all my work in the morning. And then that tall one. She was late, don't you know. Oh, only a few minutes, but late nevertheless, and—"

"Aunt Grace, I'm sure Jenny isn't interested in the foibles of past secretaries." Martin smiled at Jenny and she felt some of the tension drain away.

Glenn slammed down his fork and pushed his half-empty plate back. Tossing his napkin on the table, he shoved his chair back. "That Sam Alger's cooking is a criminal offense!"

"Criminal? Oh, no, dear." Mrs. Hamilton refolded her napkin carefully. "The employment office gets references, don't you know. Martin told me so."

"That's right, Aunt Grace." Martin turned to Glenn. "And if you think it's easy to get help on the island, Glenn, then you handle the hiring. Let me tell you, it's a real pain. And besides—" Martin turned to Mrs. Hamilton "—the employment office wouldn't send a criminal—not to Aunt Grace. After all, she gives them all her business." His mouth curved lazily into a smile as he turned to Jenny. "Well, almost all. You came recommended from the university, didn't you?"

"Yes," she replied briefly. She didn't add that Mr. Williams, Aunt Blanche's old beau and Mrs. Hamilton's lawyer also had written a letter of recommendation. The tension was building again, as it had in the library before dinner, and she felt the less said the better. If this sort of atmosphere was continued, she thought, she'd be lucky to last the two and a half weeks.

"Aunt Grace is fortunate to have you," observed Martin. He looked over at Glenn. "Nice to have another pretty girl around the place, isn't it, Glenn?"

Glenn's face darkened, as if a shadow had passed over it. Abruptly he stood. "Excuse me," he said. "I've work to do." And with that, he strode from the dining room. By now, Jenny felt the meal had been nothing short of a disaster. The blatant references to secretaries coming and going, the tense atmosphere, the two nephews with their polarized views on the disposition of the island—to say nothing of their polarized dispositions—all combined to make her feel exceedingly uneasy. One thing she did know. She was going to remain neutral. She had no intention of taking the side of either nephew. And that, she thought grimly, was not going to be easy.

Mrs. Hamilton interrupted her thoughts. "Come, Jenny," she said, rising to her feet. "We'll adjourn to the library and lay our plans for tomorrow morning's work. Excuse us, please." She motioned for Jenny to follow. The others stood as they walked from the dining room into the hall. "I like to get an early start." She tossed the words over her shoulder as her high heels clicked on the parquet floor down the hall to the library. She stepped aside for Jenny to enter first and then closed the door behind her. Going directly to her desk, she began pulling folders and papers and over-size envelopes from the drawers. "I haven't gotten around to filing these yet."

She thrust them at Jenny. "Look them over. There are some deeds and papers on water rights and . . . I can't just dump them on the historical society. I must have some order to them first." She pulled out a bulging folder with a rubber band around its middle. "Here, just put all those papers in this file. It's sort of a funny file, don't you know. Anything I don't know what to do with, I stick in here."

Jenny slipped the rubber band off and laid the papers inside the folder. "Perhaps I can devise a more exact filing system," she ventured, but Mrs. Hamilton was already reaching for the two-drawer file beside her desk.

She pulled on the drawer. "Oh, dear. I forgot. I didn't bring my key." She sat back in the chair and sighed. "Someone ransacked my files a couple of weeks ago, so now I keep them locked."

"Broke into your files?" exclaimed Jenny, surprised. "What were they looking for?" Surely nothing could be found in this chaos, and obviously there was no money or jewelry locked away here.

"I don't know. Perhaps it was just curiosity. That tall secretary was snoopy." Mrs. Hamilton's lips pursed. "No other word for her—just snoopy!" She looked embarrassed. "I'm sorry, Jenny. I shouldn't burden you with such unladylike comments. Thank goodness those boxes weren't disturbed. I don't know exactly what we'll find in them, but they're stuffed full of papers. I thought we'd start with the files and then go on to the boxes." She frowned and her finger began to twirl the strand of hair. "I do try to be organized. I wish I had my key."

"You can show me the files in the morning, Mrs. Hamilton. Now what time would you like me to start work?"

"Eight-thirty. Breakfast is served from seven until eight." Mrs. Hamilton stood up. "I'm glad you're here, Jenny. I have a good feeling about you. I'm sure we're going to get along fine."

"I'm sure we will." Jenny snapped the rubber band around the file with a flourish. Maybe, just maybe, this job was going to work out. It had to.

"Frankly, I'll be glad to get all these papers to the historical society and deed this place to the state when I'm gone." She sighed. "It's been difficult making this decision. Each boy wants me to do something different, but I know my responsibility. By giving the island back to the state, I am making retribution for Grandfather."

Jenny must have looked mystified, for Mrs. Hamilton, by way of explanation, added, "Clayborn, don't you know." Shoving the chair under the desk, she held on to the back of it. "If only I could make the boys happy! Glenn wants me to keep the island in the family, give the historical papers to the society and allow controlled development—housing and recreational sites—on the island. But Martin wants to preserve the island as is. He's a conservationist, don't you know." She hesitated a moment. "I wish he wouldn't goad Glenn. But he always has been a tease and Glenn doesn't always take it too well. Especially since he brought a special girl to the island four or five years ago and Martin jokingly made a play for her. Unfortunately the girl responded, and Glenn has been ... well, testy with Martin ever since." She reached across the desk and pushed a framed picture toward Jenny. "Here. These are the boys when they were four and almost six."

No one could have missed who the children were. Even then Glenn had been dark and intense-looking. He was gripping the back of a chair as if he were responsible for holding it together. Martin, though, was at ease. He was leaning back in the chair, hands folded in his lap, smiling at the camera. "They're handsome children, Mrs. Hamilton."

She studied the picture for a moment. "They're like my own, don't you know. They have always lived here. Merci, my sister, and Anthony Larabie were married right here on the island and both boys were born here. Of course, Anthony had already deserted Merci when Glenn was born ... and then the boating accident ..." Her voice was almost a whisper and finally faded away into her thoughts.

Jenny stood by the desk not knowing whether to speak, leave or simply wait. Mrs. Hamilton's head was bowed. The clock struck its first chime for eight o'clock.

"Good heavens! Eight o'clock. I retire at eight-thirty and read until nine-thirty. There is television in the living room, Jenny, or choose a book from these shelves."

"I think I will take a book up with me. I'm going to bed, too. It's been a long day and I want to be ready to begin work tomorrow."

"Grand, my dear." Mrs. Hamilton reached out and patted her hand. "Are there any questions?"

Jenny hesitated a moment, then asked, "Why does Lone Willow have two names?"

"Two names? Oh, you mean 'Ruthie' and 'Lone Willow'?"

"Yes, Mrs. Hamilton. What do I call her?"

"'Lone Willow,'" replied the woman promptly. "That's her Indian name. Martin gave her the name of 'Ruthie' when she first came to live with me. He said it was time Indians accepted American ways—including names. He felt it would make her more a part of our society, don't you know." Mrs. Hamilton flicked off the desk light.

"But you call her 'Lone Willow'?"

"I'm of the older generation, dear. I'm not as confident as Martin that our part of society merits the Lone Willows." Her voice caressed the name. "Glenn and Martin love Lone Willow like a sister, but they disagree as to which culture she should emulate." She was quiet a moment, then added, "When she first came, four or five years ago, she liked being called 'Ruthie.' So Glenn and Martin and even Bobby Black Bear obliged, but this last year she has become interested in her heritage and prefers her Indian name. Now only Martin calls her 'Ruthie.'" Mrs. Hamilton laughed. "Of course, Bobby Black Bear forgets on purpose sometimes, just to tease, and calls her 'Ruthie.' He likes her."

Jenny nodded. "Thank you, Mrs. Hamilton. I won't delay you any longer."

"Good night. I hope you rest well."

"May I take this folder up with me? Perhaps I could look it over tonight."

Mrs. Hamilton opened the door. "Fine. But don't stay up too late. These papers have been around and in a mess for years. One more day won't hurt, don't you know." She lingered at the doorway for a moment. "Just switch off the lights when you finish, Jenny. Good night."

"Good night, Mrs. Hamilton." Jenny glanced at the bookshelf, then decided she was too tired to start a book. She switched off the light. Closing the door to the library and clutching the file close to her, she headed down the hall to the stairs. The door to the living room was closed, as was the dining room door. The hall stretched ahead of her like a poorly lit tunnel. Her footsteps echoed on the bare floor and twice she turned around thinking someone was behind her. She had a dreadful urge to run.

When she reached the stairs she stopped, heart pounding. She glanced back down the hall. Someone *was* following her, she was sure. Then she saw the shadowy form at the end of the hall. It seemed to fill the narrow passageway and floated like a black balloon toward her.

When it reached the center of the hall, she saw the overhead light shining on his bald head. She didn't know whether to run or laugh with relief.

"Mr. Alger?"

"Yeah. It's me. Why are you here?"

"Why?" Jenny opened her mouth to explain, then stopped. She would have thought it was pretty obvious she was going up to her room. Besides, she didn't owe him an explanation. But she didn't want to make any enemies either.

He had moved toward her and was now standing right in front of her. Her hand felt slippery on the banister and her heart pounded with anger and fear. There was something decidedly threatening about this man. "I was hired to do a job," she said stiffly. "Just like you."

"Well, Miss Fancy Secretary," he sneered, "we'll get along jest fine if you mind your own business. No one likes a meddler. Understand?"

There was only one way to deal with this. "Good night, Mr. Alger," she said, and turned and started up the stairs.

"Mind your own business . . . or else . . ." His raspy voice followed her as she continued on her way.

The bottom step creaked. Was he following her? She made those two flights of stairs in record time. She never looked back.

CHAPTER FOUR

JENNY WAS ALMOST GASPING for breath by the time she reached her room. She breathed a huge sigh of relief and collapsed on the edge of the bed. What on earth had Alger been talking about, she wondered. Meddler? Meddler in what? She had no idea. And how ridiculous to be frightened of that fat little man. With his bulk he couldn't make it up two flights of stairs in a dead run. Or could he? Rising, she walked swiftly over to the door and locked it, just in case.

Slipping off her shoes, she kicked them into the closet. Her best bet, she decided, was to stay well clear of Mr. Alger. She reached for a hanger, and froze. Was that a noise she'd heard? Yes, there it was again, a tapping followed by a scraping sound. And again she was sure it was coming from the virgin's bedroom. Jenny was barely breathing now, straining to hear. Silence greeted her efforts. Could that horrid Sam Alger have gotten into that room someway? No, of course not. The only entry was through her room, the parents' room. Quietly she edged toward the door leading to the virgin's bedroom and turned the knob. Locked. Naturally. What a fool she was, imagining noises just because a cook glared at her. She rattled the knob in disgust.

THE NEXT MORNING she was waiting at the library door when Mrs. Hamilton, precisely at eight-thirty, bustled down the hallway, high heels clicking.

"Good morning, Jenny. I hope you slept well. Have you had breakfast?"

"Yes, Mrs. Hamilton." She followed her into the library. "I'm ready to begin work. I glanced through these papers last night. There are some interesting clippings and memorabilia. I'm sure the historical society will be delighted to receive them."

"Yes, I think so." Mrs. Hamilton unlocked her file cabinet. Pulling a bulky folder from the drawer, she said, "Now the first thing I think you should do, Jenny, is familiarize yourself with these files. I tried to get the last secretary, the snoopy one, don't you know, to do that, but . . ." Her voice trailed off as she studied one of the papers in the folder. She looked up, her eyes bright and twinkling. "I didn't know Grandma Clayborn put Four Star Hennessey Brandy in her mincemeat." She handed the folder with the papers in it to Jenny. "See. She scribbled the recipe on the back of this blank water rights agreement."

The folder was labeled Treaty Rights. Whoever had filed the recipe had either had a sense of humor or figured a firewater recipe belonged in a Treaty Rights folder. If this was an example of the filing system, Jenny could see it would take a great deal longer than three hours a day to bring order to the historical papers.

At ten-thirty Lone Willow appeared with coffee and sliced oranges. "Coffee break, Mrs. Hamilton." Her hair was braided and wrapped around her head, accentuating her high cheekbones. Delicate silver earrings dangled, and again she wore the clacking porcupine quill necklace.

"Already, Lone Willow?" Mrs. Hamilton sighed. "Time goes so fast." She cleared a spot on the desk for the refreshment tray. "We'll take a fifteen-minute break, Jenny." Pouring the coffee, she handed the cup to Lone Willow.

Without looking at Jenny, Lone Willow passed her the cup of coffee. Jenny could feel her antagonism. Did Lone Willow feel threatened by her, a girl just a few years older than she? Or was it a matter of racial protection. "I won't like you first because I know you won't like me" sort of thing; or was it a general resentment or suspicion of secretaries? That, at least, would be normal for this island. Lone Willow took coffee for herself and sat in the other easy chair.

"Did Glenn speak to the new cook about our schedule?" Mrs. Hamilton asked.

"Yes, lunch will be at twelve-thirty and dinner at six-thirty. Glenn even wrote out the schedule and Scotch-taped it to the refrigerator."

"Fine, Lone Willow. Now about dinner." Mrs. Hamilton looked questioningly at her.

"The menu is as you planned." Lone Willow smiled. "And I won't bring last-minute vegetables for Mr. Alger to cook tonight."

Mrs. Hamilton laughed. "My, weren't those carrots tough! Nutritional, don't you know, but tough."

Lone Willow nodded, her eyes lighting up as she looked at Mrs. Hamilton. She really cares for the woman, thought Jenny, not just as her employer, but with a deeper regard.

"Have you finished your first lesson yet?" Mrs. Hamilton reached for an orange section, then held the plate out for them.

Lone Willow shook her head. "No, but I'll get to it this afternoon." She laughed, a trilling sound that matched the soft lilt of her voice. "Don't worry about my correspondence course, Mrs. Hamilton. I'll do it."

"I am concerned, Lone Willow. I want you to enter the university this fall." Turning to Jenny, she added, "American history is the only requirement she's missing."

"I'm a history major, Lone Willow," Jenny said. "If I can help you in any way, let me know."

Lone Willow turned quickly toward her, eyes shining. For a moment Jenny thought she had finally broken the barrier and Lone Willow was going to accept her as a friend. But as quickly as the young woman brightened, she sobered. With a slight nod, she murmured, "Thank you." Rising to her feet, she carried her cup to the tray. "I'll get it done, Mrs. Hamilton. Honest."

After Lone Willow left, Mrs. Hamilton explained that for the past four summers Lone Willow had worked for her as housekeeper-companion. She was an orphan, reared by foster parents since she was seven. When she turned sixteen, she had applied for full-time summer work. "And after that first summer," Mrs. Hamilton said in a loving tone, "I knew that she deserved all the aid I could give her. She was helpful, eager to please, and happy—oh, so happy. She finished high school commuting by boat to the mainland, and by this spring had completed two years of junior college, except for American history." Mrs. Hamilton's gray-green eyes overflowed. "Lone Willow fills many voids for me—those left by my sister's death. She's like the daughter I never had." Her fingers played with the strand of hair. "An excellent employee, too." She glanced at Jenny, her lip trembling. In a quiet voice, she added, "Lone Willow is a friend, a true friend." A smile, warm and loving, lightened the lines in her face and the tense, time-scheduled Mrs. Hamilton momentarily disappeared.

Lone Willow was fortunate to have a friend like Mrs. Hamilton. Once again Jenny felt the keen loss of her parents. They had been friends, too. Her loneliness wasn't a sharp hurt, but a by now familiar utter emptiness.

They worked until eleven forty-five. Jenny had begun sorting out the folders and had papers in stacks surrounding her on the floor.

"Oh, dear, it's time to quit for the day. I'm sure this watch must run faster some days." Mrs. Hamilton leaned back in the desk chair and stretched her arms above her head. "You know, Jenny, I finally feel that with your help I'm going to get these papers in order. It's a good feeling."

"I'm sure we will," Jenny assured her, feeling warm and confident inside. "Would it be all right if after lunch I come back and pile these stacks of paper in one place? It'll make it easier to begin work tomorrow."

Mrs. Hamilton twirled her hair around her fingers, not answering at once, not even looking down at Jenny, surrounded by paper piles. "Of course." She smiled. "I'm glad you're interested in the work." Her voice wavered. "But . . . I'm not really as difficult to please as you might surmise."

"Oh, no, Mrs. Hamilton, I don't think that." Jenny climbed to her feet. "It's just that I've sorted them and I don't want them scattered. And really, I'd like to work a little while after lunch."

"Grand." She stood up and slipped her arm through Jenny's as they walked toward the door. "I have a one-track mind." She stopped and, dropping Jenny's arm, stepped in front of her blocking the doorway. "I have to get those papers in order. Help me, Jenny." Her voice was little more than a desperate whisper. "It's my duty, don't you know, to return the land to its heirs, the people." She reached out and grabbed Jenny's arm, her fingers digging into her flesh, then released her hold and, half laughing, added, "Goodness me, I'm being melodramatic. It's just that I know what I have to do and you—you seem so sincerely interested in my project and competent, it makes me eager to get the job done. Come, dear. Let's wash for lunch.''

They walked down the hall toward the stairway. On the bottom step Mrs. Hamilton turned. "I'm glad you're here, Jenny. Not only because I can see you're an efficient worker, but I feel I can trust you. You're not like that last secretary, don't you know.'' She headed up the steps, not pausing once to catch her breath.

And I don't have morning sickness like the other one, Jenny thought, warming inside with the pleasure of being appreciated, if only because she wasn't snoopy or pregnant. She followed Mrs. Hamilton up the stairs. Mrs. Hamilton was a charming lady, Jenny thought, and pleasant to work for. Why, then, did she have this cold, uneasy feeling in the pit of her stomach? She had been surprised by the note of desperation in Mrs. Hamilton's voice. It was almost as though the woman were afraid. But afraid of what? Or could it be whom? And why? Did it have anything to do with Mr. Alger's warning to Jenny to mind her own business? No, surely that wasn't possible. He hadn't been long on the island himself. But something was definitely wrong on the island, and although Jenny had no idea what it might be, she was distinctly uneasy at the thought that she was trapped on the island, with no quick way out.

Neither Glenn nor Martin were at lunch. Lone Willow explained that Glenn had gone to Shadow Cove to see Bobby Black Bear and Martin had taken a sack lunch and gone hiking.

"What are your plans for this afternoon?" Mrs. Hamilton reached across the table and patted Lone Willow's hand.

"Shall I tell you what you want to hear?" Lone Willow's black eyes sparkled and there was a trace of laughter in her voice.

Playfully Mrs. Hamilton slapped at her hand. "All right, Lone Willow, I'll stop nagging you on that correspondence course. You'll get it done. I know you will."

"Honest, Mrs. Hamilton, I'm going to work on it right after I check with Mr. Alger. I want to be sure he understands Glenn's note about meal schedules."

"Well, then, girls, if you'll excuse me, I'll rest for a little while." Mrs. Hamilton motioned for them not to stand and in a few minutes they heard her going upstairs.

"Does she stay in her room all afternoon?" Jenny asked.

"Sometimes. Would you care for more coffee?" After Lone Willow had poured it, she rolled her napkin, tucking it through the ring. "Sometimes Mrs. Hamilton spends the afternoon in her room reading, watching television, writing letters, and at other times she rests for an hour or so and then walks. There are many beautiful paths to follow on the island."

"Maybe you could show me," Jenny ventured, but again Lone Willow retreated behind her inscrutable mask.

"Just take a path and walk. You won't get lost. Now if you'll excuse me, I must speak with Mr. Alger and get on with my chores.'' Lone Willow began to clear the table.

Feeling dismissed, Jenny headed for the library. She could hear Lone Willow talking to Mr. Alger, laying down the law as to the dinner hour. Jenny waited at the doorway to hear Mr. Alger's reply. ''Lone Willow, huh?'' he snarled unpleasantly. ''Oughta change it to 'Squawking Girl.' All right. All right. Six-thirty.''

For such a slender, young girl, Lone Willow carried clout, Jenny thought, amused by her soft, lilting voice sounding so firm and full of authority. She opened the door to the library.

''Oh, no!'' The exclamation burst from her as she stopped in the doorway, unable to believe the sight. Her neat stacks of paper were scattered over the library as if a fan had whirled them about.

''Is something wrong?'' Lone Willow had hurried to her side and now stood in the doorway. ''Oh, what happened?'' She stared at the mess. ''I heard you cry out and thought you were sick or something.''

''I had these all sorted. A whole morning's work blown away.'' Jenny felt like crying. ''A window must have been left open.'' She glanced around, but the windows were closed.

''It would have to have been a hurricane to make this mess,'' Lone Willow said, then added in a whisper, ''or someone looking for something special. It's happened before.''

''The snoopy secretary?'' Jenny asked.

Lone Willow hesitated a moment, then answered, ''Well, she didn't exactly mess up the files, but I found her in here going through the files one night when everyone was in bed. Then later, when Glenn caught her going through Mrs. Hamilton's dresser drawers, they let her go.''

''Have Mrs. Hamilton's files been disturbed since?'' Jenny asked.

Again Lone Willow hesitated before answering, in low tones. ''Yes. Someone messed up her files not more than a week or so ago. Now she keeps them locked.'' Then, as though trying to cover up her apprehension, Lone Willow looked at Jenny and smiled. ''The breeze does get strong here on the island and probably someone accidentally opened a window.''

''Who?'' queried Jenny sharply, realizing she was snapping but unable to stop herself. Now she was angry. Angry that someone had wantonly destroyed her work; angry that in twenty-four hours she had been resented, discouraged and frightened; angry that someone was jeopardizing her job, her thesis, her master's degree, her bread and butter. Angry that Lone Willow knew as well as she did that Mrs. Hamilton had had an intruder and yet still tried to chatter away the implications. Why? Was she protecting someone?

''I'm sorry, Jenny,'' said Lone Willow quietly. ''Could we get this straightened up before Mrs. Hamilton comes down for cocktails, do you think? She would be so upset.''

Jenny looked at her anxious face, filled with concern, and then at the scattered papers. ''We can try, Lone Willow.''

All afternoon they picked up, sorted, stacked. Lone Willow was obviously grateful that they were trying to bring order to the library before Mrs. Hamilton saw the mess and she was a fast worker. At first they had worked silently, but as the afternoon passed, she gradually became more friendly and talkative. She told Jenny about Glenn's sales job based in Los Angeles and how he went all over the country, bidding on property. "But every chance he gets he comes back to the island, sometimes for two or three weeks at a time," she said.

"How about Martin?" Jenny asked, rubber-banding another set of papers.

"He teaches in Risco and commutes to the mainland. Bobby Black Bear does the same with his job—commutes." Lone Willow stood and carried another stack to the file cabinet. "Do you know that Bobby Black Bear and Martin went to kindergarten together and all the way through high school?"

Jenny tried to visualize shortened versions of the two men carrying their lunch buckets to school and gave up, laughing.

"Apparently the two of them used to tease Glenn and call him 'baby' because he's a year younger." Jenny was delighted that Lone Willow seemed to have opened up and had now apparently accepted her as a friend. And what a difference it made! The normally impassive face was animated now, and the eyes sparkled with life.

"Glenn and Bobby Black Bear seem so close now," observed Jenny.

"Yes." Lone Willow shook her head. "They've been close since I've known them. Mrs. Hamilton told me that Glenn and Martin had trouble over a girl."

Jenny bit her tongue to keep from asking if Glenn had a girl now. She was disgusted with herself even for thinking about it. Just because the warmth of his smile would melt a glacier was no reason to admit, either to herself, or to anyone else, any interest in him. Especially considering his rudeness on the dock and his unpleasant manner at the dinner table. Come to think of it, she pitied any girlfriend he might have, and besides, it was no business of hers.

As the afternoon wore on, Lone Willow opened up more and more. She told Jenny how Mrs. Hamilton had taken her into her home. "I love Mrs. Hamilton," she added. "She's sweet and concerned about others." She slapped a folder down on the table. "It just makes me so...so mad that someone would distress her by messing up her papers. And—" Lone Willow lowered her voice "—and make her afraid." She looked down at the papers before her.

"Afraid?" Jenny echoed. So she had been right in sensing a fear in her employer. "Of what or whom? And why?"

"I don't know," replied Lone Willow quickly, too quickly Jenny thought, to be entirely truthful.

"Maybe I can help, Lone Willow," she urged. "After all, two heads are better than one. Why is Mrs. Hamilton afraid?"

"I don't know. Honest," replied the young woman. "But I have a hunch the 'why' deals with the disposal of this island. There's a treaty that gives ten feet up from the lake to the Indians. That means that all the homes around the lake using the waterfront for docks and cabanas don't even own the land those docks and cabanas are built on." She shrugged. "Of course, the island isn't exactly lake frontage, I don't think."

Jenny recalled the many docks she'd seen on the boat ride to the island. What a mess if the Indians decided to enforce the treaty and use the ten feet of lake frontage for themselves.

"Whatever Mrs. Hamilton does with the island, leave it to the state as a public park or will it to Glenn or Martin or both, it doesn't affect anyone except Glenn and Martin. And they wouldn't mess around with their aunt's files, surely? So who could it be? A mysterious John Q. Citizen?" Even as she said it, another possible solution dawned on her. Why not Bobby Black Bear? It wouldn't be unreasonable for him to be interested in finding some old treaty or agreement that would give the island to the Indians.

For some moments Lone Willow was silent; busily opening the file drawer and putting in another stack of papers. Then she turned and faced Jenny. "Martin and Glenn both love their aunt. Neither of them would do anything to upset her. And Bobby Black Bear loves her, too. Besides, he wouldn't be interested. He has his property on the island now."

Half laughing, Jenny said, "That leaves the mysterious John Q. Citizen as the culprit. Unless you think Mr. Alger sneaked in here. But why?"

Lone Willow shook her head. "He couldn't have. When you and Mrs. Hamilton left to wash up for lunch, I was in the kitchen helping Mr. Alger get the meal on the table. He didn't have the opportunity."

"He doesn't have a motive, either," Jenny pointed out. "At least, I can't possibly think of one."

It was close to five o'clock and the work was finally completed. They were about to leave, when Glenn came in, dressed in a gold warm-up suit. He walked right up to Jenny and reached for her hand. "Hey, Jenny, I'm sorry about being rude on the dock yesterday. I thought you were another simpleton that Martin had hired. He certainly hasn't been too efficient so far! Aunt Grace told me this afternoon how efficient you are...." He stopped and looked down at her. "Am I forgiven?"

At that moment she'd have forgiven him if he were Jack the Ripper. He looked so utterly different; a little contrite, perhaps, with a faintly wry smile, but above all, warm and caring. "Nothing to forgive, Glenn," she said simply. Not now, anyway, she thought, noticing irrelevantly how the gold of his warm-up suit set off his deep tan and matched the flecks in his dark eyes. There was no doubt he was one of the most confusing men she'd ever met, and certainly the most infuriating.

"How was Bobby Black Bear?" Lone Willow asked.

"I don't know. I didn't make it to his place. Got to working on the boat and sunbathing and the day was gone." He smiled at Jenny. "Guess I thought you'd be relaxing on the dock your first day, Jenny."

"Tomorrow, maybe," she returned briefly, her mind working furiously. She didn't look at Lone Willow. She was afraid her knowing look would show. If Glenn hadn't gone to Bobby Black Bear's, after all, then he had had the opportunity to mess up Mrs. Hamilton's papers. And as a possible inheritor of the island, he certainly had the motive. Mentally she shook her head. It couldn't have been Glenn. He was too fond of his aunt to hurt her in any way.

"Would you like to take a boat ride tomorrow afternoon?" Glenn's query interrupted her thoughts. "We could take a run over to Bobby Black Bear's place."

She hesitated. It would be fun, but she didn't want to compromise her position of neutrality. She had to keep a clear head and an uncommitted heart if she was to be effective in her job.

"Go on and go, Jenny," urged Lone Willow. "Bobby Black Bear would be happy to show you his place. He's very proud of it."

"All right," she agreed finally and somewhat reluctantly.

"Fine. Well, I'd better get myself cleaned up. See you later."

Lone Willow and Jenny headed for their rooms to get ready for dinner. On the stairs they met Martin. "How was your hike?" Lone Willow asked.

"Hike? Oh, I didn't go." He grinned in an embarrassed sort of way. "I've been working in the darkroom. Got some great pictures of the mountain sheep silhouetted against the sky.'' Martin was already dressed for dinner, wearing dark-blue slacks with a plaid sport shirt. ''Some afternoon maybe you'd like to hike up to the peak and see the sheep, Jenny,'' he added. ''They're an endangered species.''

''Thank you, Martin. It'd be fun.'' And it would keep things balanced between Glenn and Martin, she thought.

Neither Lone Willow nor Jenny said anything as they climbed the stairs. Jenny was sure that Lone Willow knew as well as she that now it was anyone's guess who had scattered the papers. Glenn, Martin, or even Bobby Black Bear. Each had had the opportunity. Jenny just wished she knew what they might have been searching for.

When they reached Lone Willow's room, she started to open the door, then stopped and turned to Jenny. ''I can't thank you enough, Jenny. Mrs. Hamilton would have been so upset about those papers. It was kind of you to spend your afternoon off resorting them.''

''Glad to do it, Lone Willow, and I couldn't have done it without your help.'' Jenny headed to her room.

Her mother had always said there was a silver lining to every cloud. The cloud in this case had been the messed up papers, but the cloud had had more than one silver lining. Lone Willow and she were on the way to becoming friends. And Glenn—well, at least their relationship was on a polite basis now.

CHAPTER FIVE

GLENN DIDN'T FORGET HIS INVITATION to visit Bobby Black Bear's home. After lunch the next day he followed Jenny into the hall. "Are you ready to go to BB's this afternoon? The boat ride should be nice—the lake is calm."

"Just a minute." She hurried toward the stairs. "I have to get a sweater and a scarf."

"I'll wait for you on the dock, gas up the boat." He grinned, his dark eyes sparkling. "You don't look like the sort who'd fall for the line 'out of gas.'"

"I can't walk on water, but I am a pretty good rower," she parried with a grin.

"Foiled again. See you on the dock."

She probably should work more on organizing Mrs. Hamilton's files, Jenny thought, but Glenn's invitation was too tempting. He had been chivalrous enough to apologize for being rude; it would be impolite of her to refuse his invitation. Besides, it was an opportunity to see more of the island. Glenn was obviously trying to be gracious, in which case, so would she. And he was her employer's nephew. Reaching her room, she grabbed her sweater from the drawer. But I won't take sides, she vowed silently as she hurried back down the stairs.

While she tied on the life jacket, Glenn pushed off from the dock. In a few minutes they were speeding across the lake. From the boat she saw the house perched high upon the rocky cliffs. Like a fortress it seemed inaccessible to all foes.

They followed the island shore around the point. Glenn steered the boat, relaxed and confidently, with one hand; the other rested in his lap. "When we get around this point, the trees are dead, stark and ghostly-looking things," he shouted over the noise of the motor.

She nodded in understanding, but wasn't ready for the sight that met her gaze. As they rounded the point Glenn slowed the engine down. She couldn't believe the view. Dead trees filled the cove, extending into the shallow water. Their bleached trunks and branches reached up to the blue sky like skeletons in some frozen balletic tableau.

"Good heavens! What happened to them?" she shouted over the chugging engine. "The ones in the water look as though they drowned. Is that possible?"

Glenn cut the motor and the boat rocked gently with the waves. "It looks that way, but I don't know for sure. Bobby Black Bear's grandmother, Laughing Star, used to tell him about hot springs in this cove and how the Indians long ago came here to sweat out their ailments. Hot springs would account for the dead vegetation, but there's no sign of them now."

Jenny shuddered. "It's spooky. No life. Just gray-ish-white sentinels marching into the water."

"Oh, there's life, Jenny." Glenn pointed to a tall tree on the water's edge. "See the nest at the very top. It's an eagle's nest. I've spotted five or six of them on the island. The point that this cove runs into is called 'Bird Point.' Lots of birds here. Ducks, Canada geese, wild turkeys. Seen enough?"

She nodded. They rounded Bird Point and headed toward the shore.

"This is Shadow Shallows." He shouted. "There's BB's place."

A small log house with the front screened in sat back about fifty yards from the beach. Bobby Black Bear was on the pier to meet them. Glenn cut the motor and stood up, rope in hand, to toss to him.

"Good to see you." Bobby Black Bear held out his hand to steady Glenn as he leaped to the dock. "Glad you brought Jenny."

She wanted to be as nautical as Glenn, but leap she couldn't—not with that dark water sloshing between dock and boat. She hesitated.

"Hey, Glenn, pull the boat closer," suggested Bobby Black Bear. "Jenny isn't as used to this as you are."

Glenn leaped to do as he suggested, grabbing the rope and holding it taut as Bobby Black Bear helped her out.

"Come on up to the house. I'll get us something cool to drink." Bobby Black Bear led the way along a dirt path to his home.

The house wasn't large—a living room with a stone fireplace, two bedrooms, a bath and a kitchen with a large eating area. Everything in the house was clean and polished.

While she studied the photographs on the wall—a Bobby Black Bear looking rough-and-ready in a football uniform; an older Indian woman, her braids reaching almost to her waist, sitting on a straight-backed chair; Bobby Black Bear's framed degree in forestry—Bobby Black Bear went into the kitchen, returning with lemonade.

"I'll put your drink on the table, Jenny."

"What a charming place, Bobby Black Bear. Have you always lived here?" Jenny joined him on the leather couch and reached for her lemonade. Glenn wandered restlessly around the room, picking up a book, straightening a throw rug, looking out the window.

"Yes. I was born in this house. My mother died in childbirth." He looked around the room and Jenny could feel his pride in his home.

"BB's great grandfather, Gray Wolf, and my great grandfather, Horst Clayborn, came to this island at the same time." Glenn flopped down in the chair opposite them, his long legs stretched out.

"Our families go back together a long time, Jenny." Bobby Black Bear got up and took a picture off the desk. "Here's our two grandfathers." He handed the photo to her.

She studied the tintype, searching for appropriate words. What could you say about a typical Indian with an uncreased crown hat and the mustached, affluent-looking white man?

"Grandfather Gray Wolf was an Indian scout for the army. That's where he met Mr. Clayborn. He was a lieutenant assigned to the Montana territory." Bobby Black Bear set the tintype on the desk again.

"That's why it makes me so damn mad that Martin wants to divide the blankets," explained Glenn. "Why, from the great-grandfathers through each generation, our families, Bobby Black Bear's and mine, have been friends. Now Martin comes along and wants to ignore that fact and get the island all to himself." Abruptly Glenn rose to his feet and began to pace the room, his face dark with anger.

"But I thought Martin just wanted to preserve the island, as is, undeveloped," she ventured, then stopped, feeling Glenn's anger permeating the room. "You know," she continued weakly, "keep it as a monument to the past."

"He wouldn't know the past if he fell into yesterday," snapped Glenn derisively.

"Hey, Glenn, lighten up. Jenny doesn't care." Bobby Black Bear laid a restraining hand on Glenn's shoulder.

"But I do," she protested. "I care because I'm interested, because it relates to my job of organizing the papers about these people and their doings for the historical society. And because I'm a history major, interested in the past. I do care, Bobby Black Bear."

"Then you'll help?" Glenn stood in front of her, looking down, his voice almost a whisper.

"You're putting her on the spot, Glenn. That's not fair."

"Well, my fine brave." Glenn whirled around, challenging his friend. "I'll bet Martin's already propositioned her."

"Propositioned!" Now she was angry. She was also, she realized, stalling for time. How well Glenn knew his brother!

Slowly Glenn turned to face her, his dark eyes glitteringly cold. "In a business sense, my dear, in a business sense."

She didn't answer, busying herself instead with buttoning her sweater. What could she say? Martin had indeed "propositioned" her, just the previous evening. How do I stay neutral, she wondered, with both brothers asking for my help? And if the papers were just mementos, why would Glenn and Martin be so eager for her help? There had to be something in those files. Something that would change Mrs. Hamilton's mind as to the disposition of the island....

"Come on, Jenny. I'll show you my garden." Bobby Black Bear turned to Glenn. "Coming?"

They followed him out the back door and down the steps to rows and rows of vegetables. "And over here is my orchard. I have Bing cherry trees and some apples." Bobby Black Bear pointed to the far side of the small orchard. "And there is the organic garden that I plant for Mrs. Hamilton."

"Is this where those tough carrots came from?" queried Glenn with a grimace.

"I had carrots the other night and they were great," Bobby Black Bear said. "I don't think that new cook, Alger, knows his way around the kitchen too well."

Well, he sure knows his way down a dark hall, Jenny thought, shuddering at the memory of his words: "mind your own business . . . or else."

They walked around the side of the house and down the path to the dock. Bobby Black Bear steadied her as she stepped into the boat.

"Any messages for the Hamilton household?" Glenn slid behind the wheel. "To Lone Willow, for example?" he added with a twinkle in his eye.

"Yes, tell her I'll pick her up about seven-fifteen tonight. I'm taking her to the Indian rights powwow in Risco. Should be interesting." He shoved the boat away from the pier.

In moments they were skimming across the lake. When they arrived at the Hamilton dock, Glenn tied the boat and then helped her out. "Thanks, Glenn, for the boat ride. I loved seeing Bobby Black Bear's home and garden."

Casually Glenn slipped his arm through hers and guided her toward the end of the pier, where there was a bench. "Bobby Black Bear does a good job and he's a good man. Fine family." They sat on the bench, looking out across the water. A haze hung over the now blue-green lake and the waves lapped gently against the pier and the cliffs.

"It's beautiful here," Jenny said, sighing contentedly.

"Yes. You know, I can go to Los Angeles on a job and spend several weeks or a month in tense, competitive bidding and come back here, and this place restores my spirit every time." Glenn smiled wistfully.

"We all seek a place to recharge," Jenny said. "Would you like to live here year-round—if your work permitted?"

Glenn nodded. "Yes. I'd be content. BB has the perfect setup. He works out of his home, basically, checks by phone with his mill manager but spends his working hours in the forests. Granted, it's lonely for him since his grandmother, Laughing Star, died. But he never complains. He loves Lone Willow, but she's still so young and of course, has to finish her education."

"I thought there was something between them," Jenny observed. "I felt it last night at dinner."

"Lone Willow is a lovely girl and she's good for Aunt Grace, too." Glenn looked at his watch. "Guess we'd better head for the house. Must adhere to Aunt Grace's schedule."

The sun was still warm on their backs as they strolled along. "Mrs. Hamilton speaks so fondly of Lone Willow. I'm sure she enjoys having a woman, even a young one, around," Jenny said.

"Aunt Grace still misses my mother. She loved her. They were very close." Glenn shook his head. "A real tragedy. Bobby Black Bear's father and my mother lived all their lives on the lake. They knew how treacherous it could be."

"Was it a storm?"

"No. Aunt Grace said there was no apparent reason for the boat to sink." Taking a deep breath, Glenn added, "Martin and I were lucky, though. Aunt Grace and Uncle Bradford raised us like sons. Uncle Bradford died almost eight years ago."

Now she followed Glenn along the path. The forest closed in around them, shutting out the world of historical papers, prejudices, propositions. The sun filtered through the leaves, giving the woods a lacy effect. Was it only forty-eight hours ago that she had walked with Bobby Black Bear up this path, haunted by the remoteness? It wasn't remote, she now realized, simply private. She studied Glenn, walking so straight and sure footed ahead of her. His dark-green slacks and sport shirt blended into the setting.

"How about you, Glenn?" she asked. "You've told me about Martin and Bobby Black Bear. You said you bid, but on what and where?"

"Land. I work for the National Land Development Company and bid on different parcels all over the country. We put up shopping centers, recreational facilities, subdivisions. It's exciting and always different."

They climbed the steps to the front veranda.

"Glenn, I truly enjoyed this afternoon. Thanks."

"Next time I'll make you tell me all about you." He hesitated a moment, then added, "I know I come on strong about the island. But I care. And I want Aunt Grace to do what's best for everyone."

"I understand."

"So you'll help?"

Before Jenny could answer, someone cleared his throat.

"Well, I always said you were a fast worker, Glenn." Martin stood at the bottom step, looking up at them. How long had he been standing there? Face burning, Jenny felt ashamed, as though she were a child caught with her hand in the cookie jar.

Glenn's sharp intake of breath sounded harsh in the quiet of the afternoon. "And you, I see, are up to your old tricks, Martin," he returned coldly. "Sneaking around and worming your way around people. Well, it won't work this time. Aunt Grace is too level-headed to go along with your status quo fantasy." He looked at Jenny as though waiting for her to speak.

She stood between them, silent and confused. She wanted to say something to stop the argument, but no matter what she said it would sound as if she were choosing sides.

"Please excuse me, Jenny." Now Martin looked embarrassed. He turned to Glenn. "Sorry, Glenn. I didn't mean to intrude."

"We were just going in, Martin," Jenny said evenly. "No intrusion."

"Oh, Jenny, I brought the mail over and you have a letter from Keith someone or other." Martin walked up the steps to join them on the veranda.

Immediately Glenn turned and walked away.

"Hey, Glenn, old boy, I said I was sorry," Martin called after him.

Glenn made no reply. Opening the front door, he strode into the house. The door slammed behind him, fairly vibrating with his anger.

"Jenny, I'm sorry. Guess I blew it." Martin's voice was low and contrite. "But I have as much at stake in this island as he does and I guess I can get pretty worked up about it, too. It brings out the worst in me."

She smiled. "Don't worry about it. Just remember that I'm simply Mrs. Hamilton's secretary. I can't side with either of you."

But Martin still appeared troubled. He studied the porch floor, then looked up at her, a wry expression on his boyish face. "Glenn has a reputation for being quick-tempered. I guess I should know better than to confront him."

Being in complete agreement with this statement, Jenny felt there was little she could say. It had been an uncomfortable few minutes, the like of which she hoped she would not witness again. She shrugged. "Guess I'll pick up my letter and clean up for dinner," she said.

"The mail is on the hall stand," Martin told her.

Hurrying into the house, she sorted through the mail on the stand and claimed Keith's letter.

LATER SOAKING IN THE TUB, she thought about Keith. She lay relaxed, waiting—almost hoping—for a glow or spark to envelop her. It would be so much simpler to love dependable, predictable Keith. But she didn't love him and never had.

Apparently he was working on a sales promotion idea he hoped he could sell to his father. Fat chance, she thought wryly. He hadn't been able to sell his father on letting him continue school or choosing his own profession. Keith had been an anthropology major and had hoped to continue his education after college, but his father had soon put an end to that idea. "I've got diamonds and rubies in the store," he'd said. "More than you'll ever find in any King Tut tomb. Time to stop digging and start working." The only digging Keith was going to get, Jenny thought, was of his own grave of frustration and unhappiness. Her parents had been so different, urging her to make decisions and plan her own life. Keith had loved his anthropology studies but at his father's insistence, had stopped them. She wondered if in a few years, Keith, his ambition and hopes dormant, would be like those bare, gray trees—standing, but dead. That's unkind, she admonished herself, but, then, bribery wasn't exactly pleasant, either. Keith had written that if she'd give up her summer job and come back to Missoula and marry him, his parents would finance the remainder of her college training.

She turned on the hot water faucet. In her mind she saw the last sentence in Keith's letter. "Dad is giving me next Saturday, June 23, off so I can come to the island, and hopefully we can return to Missoula together." Let's see, Jenny thought, if I left on the twenty-third, I would hold the all-time secretarial record for the shortest time in Mrs. Hamilton's employment.

She pulled the plug and stood up, reaching for the towel. Rubbing her body briskly, as if by that she could remove an unpleasant memory, she thought about the quarrel between Glenn and Martin. How angry Glenn had been at his brother's insinuations! Not that she could blame him in some ways, for he knew full well that Martin had requested her help long before he himself had. But the memory of his voice, so cold with disdain for his brother, sent a shiver down her spine. How could two brothers so close in age be so different? The boyish Martin was relaxed, courtly, easygoing and charming. Glenn, on the other hand, could be rude and arrogant, a volatile man whom, she didn't doubt, could love as fiercely as he hated. But despite the obvious flaws, she sensed in Glenn a sincerity in all his emotions that for some reason she found lacking in Martin.

The only thing they appeared to share in common, albeit for totally different reasons, was an interest that amounted almost to passion in the island. And each wanted her help. But how could she help either of them? Was there a document that would favor Glenn's hope for the island or grant Martin his plan of status quo?

Bobby Black Bear's warning drummed in her mind. "Don't take sides."

CHAPTER SIX

DRESSING FOR DINNER, Jenny wished she had brought something soft and feminine, something less secretarial. She glanced at the clock on the bedside table, checked quickly in the mirror, then hurried down stairs to the library.

The door to the library was open, but she hesitated a moment on the threshold, composing herself. She hoped Glenn was over his anger at Martin. Taking a deep breath, she walked into the room.

"Hi, Jenny. Did you have a good time?" Lone Willow, standing by the tea cart, was dressed in a beaded buckskin dress. Her long, dark hair was held in place by a matching beaded band.

"Oh, yes, Lone Willow. A perfectly lovely afternoon. Bobby Black Bear has such a nice place. By the way, he said he'd pick you up tonight at seven-fifteen for the meeting." She hesitated, then added, "But I guess you already know that—Glenn probably told you."

"Glenn?" Lone Willow lifted the lid of the ice bucket to check for ice. She shrugged. "I haven't seen Glenn since lunch. Mr. Alger said he stopped by the kitchen around five to say he wouldn't be having dinner tonight."

That figures, Jenny thought. After his quarrel with Martin, he'd obviously prefer the pleasure of his own company at dinner rather than that of his brother. She felt Lone Willow's look and hoped that her disappointment didn't show. "Am I too early?" she asked brightly.

"No. The others should be arriving any minute. I'm going to be the bartender tonight." Lone Willow's eyes sparkled. "So keep your cocktail order simple."

Dinner was served promptly at six-thirty. Glenn's absence at the head of the table seemed to act as a catalyst to Martin. He teased his aunt and joked kindly with Lone Willow. To Jenny he was as charming as usual, complimenting her on her colorful skirt and laughing at her stories of growing up. Yet still she couldn't bring herself to believe he was sincere.

"Aunt Grace," said Martin, laying his hand on Jenny's, "I thought I'd ask Jenny to do some sight-seeing with me tomorrow. How about joining us, and you, too, Ruthie. We could take a picnic." He stopped and looked over at Jenny with his usual easy smile. "That is," he added, "if Jenny will go."

She felt as if all three of them were staring at her, as though the whole idea of a picnic hinged on her decision alone. Should she go? she wondered. No doubt it would upset Glenn again, but what difference would that make? Besides, she'd spent one afternoon with Glenn. If she didn't want to get caught in the middle

of the two brothers, surely it was only fair she spend
an afternoon with Martin.

The silence lengthened, until Martin said silkily,
"Unless, of course, Glenn has staked a claim on you."

That, thought Jenny angrily, was hitting below the
belt. But she managed a somewhat grim smile and replied, "Not at all. I was just wondering if I shouldn't
spend some extra time sorting and classifying."

"Now, Jenny, we'll work in the morning as usual
and your afternoons are free. You'll enjoy Martin's
tour. I'm sorry I can't join you, but I do cherish my
couple of hours' rest, don't you know." Mrs. Hamilton folded her napkin and slipped it through the napkin ring. "Besides, I've found an old journal of
Merci's and I'm anxious to look through it."

"A journal of Mother's?" queried Martin sharply.
His hand clutched his napkin as if it were a life pre-
server. Visibly calming himself, he added, "How exciting, Aunt Grace. It must bring back fond
memories." He reached out and patted his aunt's arm;
but to Jenny his smile seemed suddenly strangely
forced. "Where did you find it?"

"In her study. I suppose I should have cleaned out
her things long ago, Martin, but I just couldn't make
myself go into that room and do it, don't you know."
Mrs. Hamilton's voice broke, and she paused for a
moment before adding, "Each fall I think I'll clear out
her things, but I go in there and then simply leave the
room as it was."

"Mother had your bedroom, Jenny, and the connecting room she used as a sitting room-study," Mar-

tin explained. He turned back to his aunt. "When did you start going through her things, Aunt Grace?"

"The other day, Monday. Or maybe it was Tuesday. I don't remember. I went in there to look for some pictures and came across her journal. At any rate, I'm looking forward to reading it and will share it with you and Glenn if it's anything more than a young woman's personal thoughts."

For a moment, Jenny was relieved that the mysterious tapping, scraping noise was finally explained. Until she realized that if the sound coming from the virgin's bedroom was caused by Mrs. Hamilton, how did she get into that room? She could have entered through the parents' bedroom, but she certainly didn't leave that way. Probably, thought Jenny, disgusted with herself, it wasn't Mrs. Hamilton or anyone else causing that clacking, scraping noise. Probably it was just a combination of her imagination and a creaky old house.

"I'm glad you found something of your sister's, Mrs. Hamilton. It'll make you remember the wonderful times you had together," Lone Willow said. "If you need help in sorting or repacking your sister's things, I'm available."

"Yes, Aunt Grace," Martin chimed in. "I'll be glad to help, too. It's great you found something of mother's, and I—and Glenn, too, I'm sure—will be anxious to see mother's journal." He stood, shoving in his chair. "It's a date for tomorrow, then, Jenny?" he asked.

"Fine. I'll be ready."

"How about you, Ruthie? Can you join us?"

"Thanks, Martin, but I really must get to that correspondence course." Lone Willow looked at Mrs. Hamilton.

"Don't look at me to discourage a worthwhile endeavor, Lone Willow." She walked around the table and put her arm around the young woman's shoulders. "I can only add my squeeze of approval." She hugged her.

"Well, Jenny, looks like it'll be the two of us." Martin edged around the table. "Aunt Grace, how about some dominoes tonight? We could play doubles."

"That would be enjoyable, Martin, dear. Do you play, Jenny?"

"I used to play with my dad a long time ago."

"Mrs. Hamilton, I'm going out this evening," said Lone Willow. "Bobby Black Bear is picking me up in a few minutes to take me to the Indian rights powwow in Risco. I'm sorry." She fingered the quills on her necklace.

"Run along, dear. No problem. We'll play something else. Hearts or gin, don't you know." Mrs. Hamilton led the way down the hall to the library.

In the end, they played rummy and Mrs. Hamilton proved herself a champion at the game. When she excused herself to go to the bathroom, Martin said, "I've been thinking, Jenny, that perhaps we'd better not mention Aunt Grace's finding mother's journal to Glenn." He sighed. "You've seen how riled up he gets over things." His fingers tapped the tabletop.

"It's not my place, Martin, to discuss family business," she said stiffly.

"Oh, no, Jenny, I didn't mean to imply you would. It's apparent you have integrity. I just didn't want Glenn to get all worked up again. I'll tell him when he's calm and relaxed."

Mrs. Hamilton returned and sat down again. "Whose deal?"

It was after eight when they heard the front door open. Mrs. Hamilton laid down her hand in a gin. "In the library, Glenn," she called out, reshuffling the cards. "Maybe Glenn will play."

Moments later Glenn sauntered into the library. "Good evening, everyone. Looks like you're having a good time." He patted his aunt's shoulder and glanced down at the score pad. "What's the matter with you two? Aunt Grace is way ahead." Taking off his jacket, he hung it over the back of a bridge chair and then sat down at the empty place.

"Care to play, Glenn?" Mrs. Hamilton gathered up the cards and shuffled them again, arching them like a professional gambler.

"As long as it's not for money," he replied with a grin. "Not the way you deal and play. I should have warned you, Jenny, about Aunt Grace's game prowess." Obviously he was over his anger.

What a relief, thought Jenny. Life was so much more pleasant when everyone got along.

"Your play, Jenny," Mrs. Hamilton said.

"Oh, sorry."

"Missed you at dinner, old boy," Martin said. "Heavy date?"

"Sure. With a realtor. Had to check some things out for my office."

"You don't have another assignment so soon, do you, Glenn?" Mrs. Hamilton asked.

"No. I'll be around for a while, Aunt Grace."

At eight-twenty-five they totaled the scores and proclaimed Mrs. Hamilton the winner.

Standing, she sighed. "Such a nice evening. Thank you. Will you put the table and chairs away, boys, and Jenny, the cards go in the cupboard below the *Harvard Classics*." She turned her head so each nephew could kiss her cheek, leaned over and patted Jenny's hand, then, gathering her skirts, hurried toward the door. "Good night. See you in the morning," she called. Her high heels clicked down the hallway just as the clock chimed eight-thirty.

"Hey, I'm hungry. Let's raid the pantry." Glenn grabbed Jenny's hand. "Coming, Martin?"

"Sure. I'm not hungry, but I'll keep you company."

Glenn opened the refrigerator, taking out cheese and milk, found crackers in the cupboard and chose an apple from the basket on the counter. "A feast." He spread it out on the kitchen table.

The telephone rang.

"I'll get it." Martin headed for the hall. "Enjoy your snacks." The door swung shut and there was silence.

"Your aunt likes to play cards." It was an inane statement but the best she could do in her confused state. Glenn's temperament changed faster than a chameleon's color. Perversely the only thing she could think of was the journal Mrs. Hamilton had found and the fact that Martin had suggested it not be mentioned for fear of upsetting Glenn. Anyway, she didn't want to be in the middle and the best way was not to repeat anything to anyone.

"I don't want to talk about Aunt Grace or card games, Jenny." Reaching across the table, he took her hand in his. "I want to tell you I enjoyed being with you this afternoon and . . ." He paused for a moment and smiled wryly before adding, "And it seems I must apologize once again for my rude behavior. I'm sorry I marched off like that. Am I forgiven?"

"Of course," she replied with a warm smile. And it was strange, she thought, how easy she found it to forgive him. No matter how rude he might be at times, she found it impossible to stay angry with him for long.

Glenn stood and began clearing the table. "How about some waterskiing tomorrow afternoon?"

"Waterskiing?" She repeated, stalling for time. She had a date with Martin tomorrow. "Glenn, I . . ."

"Anyone home?" Lone Willow breezed into the kitchen.

"Hey, Lone Willow. How was the meeting? Take any scalps?" Glenn gave the table a quick wipe with a dishcloth.

Lone Willow crinkled her nose at him. "The meeting was fabulous. A big turnout. Chief Hawk Who Soars really was exciting to hear and he was interested in where I lived and all about this island. This was his first visit to our area. He's from South Dakota." Lone Willow laughed. "Bobby Black Bear didn't like him— particularly after he offered me a job."

Laughing, Glenn tossed the dishcloth in the sink. "Where is BB?"

"Left me at the door. He has a big day tomorrow." Turning to Jenny, she asked, "How was the card game? Did Mrs. Hamilton win as usual?"

"Yes, she won, but we had fun." The telephone rang again.

"Jenny, Jenny." Martin poked his head in the doorway. "Oh, hi, Ruthie. Jenny, you're wanted on the telephone. It's your fiancé. Keith something or other."

"He's not my fiancé!" she snapped angrily.

"Sorry, Jenny. I'm just repeating what he said." Martin lolled against the doorframe.

"Excuse me. I'll be right back." Brushing past Martin, she walked stiffly to the telephone stand at the end of the hall.

It took her some time, but by the end of the phone call she believed she'd finally convinced Keith she wouldn't return to Missoula to marry him. As she hung up, she felt relieved of his pressures, but at the same time, strangely alone. There were no ties anymore. She was alone to do exactly as she wished—a worthwhile job for Mrs. Hamilton, remain neutral and gather material for her thesis.

Martin was gone when she returned to the kitchen. Lone Willow and Glenn sat at the table, talking, and Glenn, smiling, pulled out a chair for her. Apparently he had no interest in her telephone call.

"Chief Hawk Who Soars is going to do some research," Lone Willow was saying. "He says that the Treaty of 1800 and something or other gave the Indians Lone Lake including ten feet of lake frontage."

"That's common knowledge, but nobody has ever been bothered by it," observed Glenn with a shrug. "So what is he going to do? Demand that all docks be torn down and no boat houses or other buildings be allowed on the ten feet of frontage?"

Lone Willow laughed. "I don't know about all that, but he suggested that I be his personal guide. That's when Bobby Black Bear started to get upset."

Glenn threw back his head and laughed, his dark eyes sparkling. "I can just hear BB." He stood. "Think I'd better do some checking, too. Jenny, do you mind postponing the waterskiing? We ought to check out the records at the courthouse. We could leave right after lunch tomorrow."

"Glenn, I can't go tomorrow, either waterskiing or searching for records. Martin asked me to see some of the island with him tomorrow."

"Oh."

He was obviously disappointed, but at least this time he didn't go off the deep end. "Maybe the next day?" she offered.

"Well, I guess I can stand in line for your company." Turning to Lone Willow, he said, "I don't remember the other secretaries being so rushed." His voice had a light, joking quality to it.

Lone Willow acted as if she were really thinking about her answer. "They didn't have red hair, Glenn," she observed finally, a glint in her eye. "And definitely the unfriendly types."

"Enough, you two."

Lone Willow stood and started for the door. "Think I'll turn in, Glenn and Jenny. See you tomorrow." She stopped at the doorway. "Oh, Jenny, did you tell Glenn about his mother's journal?"

"Mother's journal?" he echoed, his face suddenly darkening.

"Oh-oh." Lone Willow gulped. "Guess you didn't." She proceeded to explain how Mrs. Hamilton had found the journal and planned to share it with Martin and Glenn if it were anything more than an intimate diary.

"And you said nothing?" Glenn accused, turning angrily on Jenny. "It seems our friendly secretary has chosen sides," he added sarcastically.

"Glenn, listen," she pleaded. "Let me explain."

"Explain? Oh, yes, you're good at that, aren't you? Fooled me completely. I thought you were on my side." He turned away from her and walked toward the sink.

She glanced at Lone Willow, standing silent and shocked in the doorway. "I'm sorry, Jenny," she said in a low voice. "I didn't mean to cause trouble."

Jenny shrugged, though she felt more like crying. Any trust that Glenn might have had in her was long gone now. And just when she thought that she and Glenn were beginning to get along well. Lone Willow looked stricken and Jenny reached out and touched her arm for reassurance.

"Good night, Glenn," murmured the young woman, and left the kitchen.

"Glenn," Jenny said, "this is truly a misunderstanding. Won't you listen to me?"

He stood at the sink, looking out the window. How could she talk to that back, so stiff and forbidding?

He turned around, his face bleak, his eyes now dull and lifeless. "Did Martin arrange for your hiring, too?" he asked tonelessly. "So he could have a spy in the house?"

"No, Glenn, I swear to you," she replied vehemently. "I never saw or heard of Martin until I got this job through the university." Tears of frustration, she knew, were welling up, and she fought to keep them from spilling over. "I knew nothing about the island or your family till I came here."

"Sure, Jenny. Whatever you say." His tone indicated a complete lack of interest and care and he turned away from her once more.

She was being dismissed, and in some ways she was only too happy to oblige. The past couple of hours her emotions had yo-yoed from sheer pleasure to utter humiliation. She moved toward the door, eager to escape further scathing remarks. At the doorway she stopped. "I'll see you in the morning, Glenn," she said quietly, unable to stop herself for giving it one last try.

He didn't answer, and suddenly she was angry. Who did he think he was? She was sick and tired of being the butt of his anger over the future of this wretched island. "Listen to me, Glenn Larabie," she demanded fiercely. "I didn't betray you, and for your information, I am Mrs. Hamilton's secretary, not a message carrier for you or Martin. Ever since I arrived, I've been pulled in two different directions by you and Martin, and..." Glenn had turned around now, but she didn't care. "And I'm not a wishbone," she finished in a rush. Whirling around, she stormed out of the kitchen before he could reply. She hurried up the stairs to her room. Once there she realized she was far too angry even to think about sleeping. She'd get a book from the library and read until the words blotted out this whole fiasco, she thought, heading back down the stairs.

Quickly she chose a book from the library shelf. As she passed the closed living room door on her way back up the stairs, a voice coming from the living room stopped her. She listened.

"Money to make money. There has to be some sort of record. Maybe in that damn journal. Don't act lily-livered now. We're in too deep."

It was Mr. Alger's voice, but who was with him? Breathlessly she waited for an answering voice. Then she heard footsteps approaching and hurried up the stairs to the first floor landing. When she looked over

the railing to the hall below, she saw Glenn. He must
have been the one with Mr. Alger, but what had they
been talking about?

CHAPTER SEVEN

SUNLIGHT BRIGHTENED THE ROOM. Reluctantly Jenny opened one eye, then the other, trying to wake up. Slipping out of bed, she padded across the floor to close the window. The air was fresh, smelling of a brand-new day. The lake below was glass smooth. If only her life could be so, she thought wearily. She hadn't slept well, tossing and turning for much of the night as she mulled everything over in her mind. She had to keep this job and her responsibility must be to Mrs. Hamilton. She hadn't been hired to carry tales to either Glenn or Martin. Feeling somewhat more cheerful and more optimistic at the sight of the glorious morning, she dressed and hurried down for breakfast.

"Good morning, Jenny. You look full of energy." Martin stood, holding the chair for her.

"Are we the only ones up?" she asked, noting Glenn's absence with a sinking feeling.

"Yes. Ruthie and Glenn have gone to Bobby Black Bear's and are then going on to the mainland. Glenn said he had to check again with his office. Ruthie has to get some books from the library for her correspondence course." Martin passed the sweet rolls. Jenny helped herself at the sideboard to cantaloupe and coffee.

"Has Mrs. Hamilton eaten, too?" It was only seven-thirty.

"I think she beat Mr. Alger down," replied Martin with a laugh. "She's gung ho on that journal of mother's. She looked as if she'd read all night. She'll probably show it to you." He leaned across the table and patted Jenny's hand. "You will let me know if it's well—worth reading, interesting. I'd like to know my mother better, even if only through her journal."

So far, she thought, remaining neutral was the hardest part of her job. She knew Martin meant well, but once again he was asking her to take sides. She didn't answer him.

They ate in silence. She thought about Mr. Alger's comments she'd overheard from the living room last night. He had certainly sounded sure of himself, not like an employee at all. And Glenn? What had he been doing with Mr. Alger?

Tucking her napkin in the ring, she rose. "Excuse me, Martin. Better get to work."

"I'll have our picnic ready for this afternoon, Jenny. I'm sure you'll enjoy the trip. I'm looking forward to showing you the island. And I know you'll appreciate the majestic beauty."

Martin had an easygoing charm she found refreshing in this household of moody people. She doubted it went much deeper than the surface, but she was looking forward to the picnic. At least she could be sure her host would be polite.

When she opened the library door, she was shocked at Mrs. Hamilton's appearance. As Martin had said, the woman looked as though she'd read all night. Dark circles edged her red-lined eyes and her voice quivered as she greeted Jenny. "Good morning, dear. You look bright and fresh." The journal lay like a curse on the desk in front of her.

Mrs. Hamilton was obviously very much upset, and Jenny wondered what could possibly be in the journal to worry her so much. Some long forgotten scandal? Some particularly fond memory, or...something pertaining to the island? Jenny suspected the latter and was full of curiosity. "Are you enjoying your sister's journal?" she asked, not wanting to pry but hoping Mrs. Hamilton would share her concerns.

Mrs. Hamilton didn't answer right away. She picked up the journal and held it close, eyes closed as though she were beseeching a higher power. "I haven't decided what to do," she admitted finally. She opened her eyes and added in a trembling voice, "Merci, my dear sister, Merci. Such a burden she bore." Her voice cracked and she couldn't go on. Laying the journal in front of her, she reached into the neck of her dress for a hankie. "I didn't sleep much last night, don't you know." She dabbed at her eyes, a sad little smile on her lips. "Shall we begin work?"

They worked in silence. The files were beginning to take shape; that is, all except the "funny file." Even though Jenny had sorted through it, filing the different papers in the appropriate files, Mrs. Hamilton still tucked anything she was uncertain about into its ever expanding sides. She'd have to go back to that when everything else was in order.

The history of Grandfather Clayborn was beginning to take shape. She had found his birth certificate, or rather a record of his birth in an old Bible. Horst Clayborn was born in 1844 in Louisiana, and after the Civil War he brought his bride, Annabell Tanner Clayborn, to the West, where he served in the United States Cavalry. During his army years he met Gray Wolf, an Indian Scout for the army. After Chief Joseph of the Nez Percé was defeated in 1877, Horst Clayborn and Gray Wolf resigned from the army and together with their families came to Lone Lake Island. Glenn was right. The two families went back a long way.

She pulled another box from the wall next to the filing cabinet, snipped the cord and began sorting, making new stacks to be integrated into the metal file cabinet. "Mrs. Hamilton, look at this tintype. It's of Mr. Clayborn and Gray Wolf, I think."

Mrs. Hamilton leaned over from her desk chair and took the picture. "Ah, yes. That's Grandfather and Gray Wolf." She studied the picture more closely. "Jenny, I think...no, I'm sure. This picture was taken on the island. Right here."

Jenny stood and walked around the desk to lean over Mrs. Hamilton's shoulder and study the tintype.

"See. They're standing just about where the dock is now, and the cliffs are on either side." Mrs. Hamilton's voice rose excitedly. "This is when they first came here before the houses or dock. My goodness,

Grandfather was a handsome man. Bobby Black Bear looks like Gray Wolf, don't you think?''

If black hair, arrow-straight tallness and high cheek bones were similar features, then Bobby Black Bear indeed looked like his grandfather. Jenny squatted on the floor again and resumed her sorting of pictures, letters, agreements, water rights.

"This is a strange document." Jenny held out the yellowed paper with the swirling, looped penmanship, now faded to a rust-colored ink. "It looks like some kind of tribal agreement, but I don't know what it's doing in Mr. Clayborn's papers."

Mrs. Hamilton studied the paper for a long time and then in a low voice said, "I think this is an Indian Land Allotment Agreement."

Jenny had read about the Allotment Act of 1877 in her history studies, but she'd never seen a document pertaining to it. She wanted to ask why it was in the family papers, but Mrs. Hamilton leaned back in her chair, eyes closed, lightly tapping her forehead with the document.

Almost as if Jenny were reviewing for a history quiz, highlights of the allotment act flashed through her mind—meant to help the Indians help themselves...the president authorized to divide Indian land holdings into individual parcels and give to every Indian a particular piece of the tribally owned land...land held in trust for twenty-five years by the government, then the Indian became legal owner with the rights and responsibilities of citizenship. If any land was left after twenty-five years, it was sold off to the non-Indian homesteaders and the Indian tribe was paid the homestead price. She remembered her history professor saying that the Indians lost thousands of acres of land on this act, to say nothing of the moneys lost on the ridiculously low pricing of the acreage sold.

Jenny went back to the box, picking out another legal-looking paper, and scanned it for filing purposes. This one was a lease agreement signed by Gray Wolf, and the lessee was Horst Clayborn. *Lessee*—Horst Clayborn? She looked at the paper more carefully. It was dated June 25, 1887. With heart pounding and mouth dry, she forced herself to reread each word, not allowing her eyes to skip a single one:

I, Gray Wolf, lease Lone Lake Island—except for ten acres in Shadow Shallows, which remain mine to do with as I see fit—to Horst Clayborn, for the sum of ten thousand dollars or five dollars an acre. All taxes and land improvements will be the responsibility of the lessee. This lease to expire in twenty-five years to date. At that time the ten acres on which Horst Clayborn will build his house will be his. Ownership of the island, with the exception of Shadow Shallow, can be renegotiated with me or my heirs. Signed, Gray Wolf.

Jenny sat back, stretching her legs in front of her, too stunned to speak. A ten thousand dollar lease! Why this land was worth two hundred thousand dollars now, at least. Was this a part of the land given to

Gray Wolf as outlined in the Allotment Act? Did Clayborn buy it after twenty-five years? Was this, perhaps, the document that Martin had referred to as "interesting information"? Did Glenn know, or Bobby Black Bear? They couldn't. Glenn surely would know that he couldn't develop the island if it wasn't his. And Bobby Black Bear would speak out if he knew. In her head she added 1887 plus twenty-five, making 1912. Oh, my gosh. Was there another lease somewhere in these boxes? Or a bill of sale?

"Mrs. Hamilton." Jenny meant her voice to be firm, professionally objective, but was afraid it sounded panic-stricken.

Mrs. Hamilton opened her eyes and smiled. "Just resting my eyes, don't you know. What is it?"

"I . . . I found this. I think it might be important." And that, she thought privately, was the understatement of the century.

Mrs. Hamilton reached for the paper. As she read the document, her hands began to tremble. Her head seemed to follow as much as her eyes the words on the paper. When she finished reading it, she raised her head and began again. It seemed an eternity before she finally laid the document down. Her fingers twirled the strand of hair just behind her ear.

"Jenny." Her voice was a whispered plea. "This can't be all. Isn't there a bill of sale or . . . a statute of limitation or something?"

Scrambling to her feet, Jenny hurried to her side. Putting her arm around the woman's shoulder, she held her tight. "I'm sure there's some explanation—

maybe in those boxes. We still have four more to go through...." She pulled up a chair close to the desk and sat down within touching distance of Mrs. Hamilton.

Mrs. Hamilton sighed. "All I wanted was to get the papers in order for the historical society and—" her voice broke "—give the island to the state." She hesitated—even her twirling fingers were still—and stared at the document before her. "You know, to me Grandpa Clayborn was a wonderful grandfather, loving, fun and generous. But I've heard tell that he was ruthless." She looked up at Jenny, her gray-green eyes begging for understanding. "But in those days, Jenny, sometimes it must have been necessary to be ruthless in order to survive in the raw country. The West brought out the ruthlessness in men, don't you know. It was the time and the place that made them that way...."

Jenny nodded, not in agreement or disagreement, but as a soothing gesture. Mrs. Hamilton's theory of time and place bringing out the savagery of men was in direct conflict with her own theory that the development of the West was influenced by the type of people who settled it—the malcontents of the East— whatever their trade or profession. But this was not the time for argument. The main thing was to comfort her. "Mrs. Hamilton, we shouldn't jump to conclusions," she said with a great deal more confidence than she felt. "Let's finish the sorting and filing. Something else is likely to turn up and explain everything."

Mrs. Hamilton stood. "All I wanted to do was give the state a gift, the island, not—" she laughed ruefully "—shake the family tree." Walking around the desk, she picked up Merci's journal and slipped the lease document inside it. When she reached the door, she turned. "Please say nothing about this to anyone, Jenny. I need to think, don't you know. And will you tell Mr. Alger to send my lunch to my room, please?"

"Yes, Mrs. Hamilton, and of course I won't say anything to anyone." She couldn't help going to her and putting her arm around her. Mrs. Hamilton wanted to do something for the state, and still she had to protect her family. She was so vulnerable. Her distress hurt Jenny.

"Have a nice afternoon." Mrs. Hamilton struggled to keep her voice steady. "You'll enjoy Martin's tour. The mountain sheep silhouetted on the cliffs are spectacular, don't you know." She opened the door, and soon Jenny heard her high heels tapping rapidly down the hall and then up the stairs.

It didn't take long to tidy up the stacks and put the loose things in the file cabinet. She had to get out of this room and into the fresh air to think. The musty, yellowed documents, stale and dead smelling, permeated her thoughts, paralyzing them as if they were embalmed. Although it was only 11:25, not time to quit by twenty minutes, she hurried down the hall and out the door to the front porch. Whatever Mrs. Hamilton had learned from Merci's journal, plus the lease they had discovered this morning, had been enough to upset the woman to the point of changing her rigid schedule.

Standing on the veranda steps, Jenny looked out across the rocky cliff to the lake below. She was drawn to it as though the water were her only means of escape. Was this attraction what a jumper off a window ledge or a bridge felt—an almost hypnotic beckoning? The house behind her represented tension and an unknown fear. She sensed the ghost of Grandfather Clayborn himself stalking her, leading her through the labyrinth of his life via personal papers and shady deals. Glenn and Martin were continuing to pressure her in their own way to take sides. Now she felt the pressure of Mrs. Hamilton's distress. Poor Mrs. Hamilton, thought Jenny sadly. She was not only her employer, but a sweet, loving, human being who only wanted what was best for everyone. And how could she, Jenny, help her? She had lost all perspective. She was seeing documents and situations with emotion, not reason. Her search through the files now was not for thesis material but for papers that would help Mrs. Hamilton.

Almost with a feeling of panic, Jenny hurried down the steps. Where to go? The dock was too far. Bobby Black Bear's was out of the question, too. She had to be ready for the picnic and she had to compose her thoughts before meeting Martin.

She could hear the lake far below, lapping against the cliffs. Now she stood behind the low guardrail on the cliff edge overlooking the gray-blue water. Monotonously the waves dipped, rose, peaked, splashed against the rocks.

Sitting on the ground in back of the guardrail, she looked out. A boat, just a tiny dot, sailed in the distance. Lone Lake was aptly named. Gazing out across the water, she felt completely alone, with no one to share her thoughts, worries, hopes. A few birds circled and swooped to the lake for their lunch.

She tossed a pebble over the rail. She felt like a flower, with everyone plucking a petal from her. *Help me, help him not. Help me, help him not.* Soon she'd be stripped bare—only a stem to be discarded. Why did Martin ask her not to mention his mother's journal to Glenn? Was it truly because he didn't want to upset his brother? And Glenn? Why did he have to be so quick to anger—to judge without even a discussion. So stubborn, yet so damned appealing, despite his perverseness of character.

It was almost noon and she should tell Mr. Alger about Mrs. Hamilton's wanting her lunch in her room. Reluctantly, she got to her feet and headed for the porch stairs. When she returned from her picnic tour with Martin, she'd corner Glenn somehow and make him listen to her. She'd show him what stubbornness was! Only in her case she liked to think it was persistence. Opening the front door, she walked into the house and headed for the kitchen.

Poking her head around the kitchen door, she called, "Mr. Alger, will you take a lunch tray to Mrs. Hamilton's room, please? She's not feeling up to par." She tried to keep her voice light, friendly, but distant.

Mr. Alger stood by the stove, stirring something in a pot. He didn't even turn to look at her. "Lunch tray? Picnics? I'm the cook, not some damn nurse or social director."

"Thank you, Mr. Alger." She ignored his griping and headed for the stairs.

"Don't get uppity with me, Ms Secretary," Mr. Alger yelled. "I know why you're here."

Glancing over her shoulder, she saw Mr. Alger, toothpick in his mouth, leaning against the kitchen doorframe. "Little Miss Busybody," he hissed.

It was like hearing a rattler. A chill slithered down her spine, and it took all her willpower not to run up the stairs, away from the threat of his venom. Like a robot, she forced each leg, tense with angry fright, to bend and walk up the steps. She resisted the impulse to look over the railing to see if Mr. Alger was following her.

Once inside her room, she turned the key in the door and flopped on the bed. It would be a relief, she thought, to get away from this house for the afternoon—help her regain her perspective.

She had just finished lacing her hiking boots, when there was a knock on her door.

"Jenny, are you about ready?" Martin called.

"I'll be right down."

"Be sure to bring a sweater. It can be cool in the shade of the forest."

She heard Martin heading down the stairs. In a few minutes she joined him at the front door. He carried a basket covered with red gingham cloth.

"Feel like Red Riding Hood!" Martin queried with a smile, swinging the picnic basket.

She laughed. "So long as you're not the wolf."

He leered theatrically.

Jenny laughed. "I'm afraid your wolf imitation is not very threatening." She followed him as they headed down the path toward the dock.

"Are we going by boat? I thought this was a hiking tour." Her boots felt hot and heavy, hardly what she'd wear for a boat ride.

"Part way, but you'll get plenty of hiking in."

At the dock he handed her a life jacket and slipped one on himself. Helping her into the boat, he went back to the boathouse for the extra can of gas. She glanced over the edge of the boat down into the black depths. The boulders, tilted, ancient, remnants of the past, reminded her of Mrs. Hamilton's out-of-joint papers, mysterious and threatening.

In a few minutes Martin returned with the gas, started the motor and headed the boat toward the middle of the lake. They skimmed across the water, cutting through it and sending up silvery sprays. As they sped farther and farther from the island, she felt the tension easing out of her. She enjoyed the speed of the boat, the vivid blue of the lake and the bright sun in the clear sky. Whitecaps like ruffled lace edged the gentle waves. She leaned back against the seat, marveling at the changeability of the lake. It was a moody lake—gray with yesteryears, sometimes bright blue pulsing with life, and always dark with mystery.

Now Martin turned the boat to follow the contour of the island. They passed the cove with the dead trees and Bird Point and Shadow Shallows, Bobby Black Bear's place.

"Not much farther," Martin shouted.

They rounded the island. She figured they were almost opposite the lodge, when Martin steered toward the shore. The trees, pine and tamarack, grew close to the beach, leaving only a narrow strip of pebbled sand on which to land.

Martin slowed the boat to minimum speed and pointed to the white outcroppings protruding high above the trees. Handing her the binoculars, he motioned for her to look. She adjusted the lens and studied the bleached rock, now seemingly close. She hoped she'd see a Bighorn sheep silhouetted on the crags, but nothing.

After Martin secured the boat, he lifted the picnic basket out and, carrying it in one hand, took hers in the other. Together they started up the path winding up from the beach. As they walked deeper into the silent forest, the sound of their boots on the pine needles and pebbles was amplified, so that the climb sounded like an army patrol breaking through the brush. After they had hiked about fifteen minutes, losing sight of the rocks periodically as they dipped into meadows and then seeing them again closer as they reached the top of a knoll, Martin stopped.

"How about some lunch, Jenny? It's shady here in the glen." Setting the basket down, he spread out the gingham cloth and then took out fried chicken, potato salad, carrot sticks, brownies and two apples.

After lunch Martin lay back with his arms under his head.

"A delicious lunch." Jenny tried to keep the amazement out of her voice.

"Yes, thank goodness Ruthie took charge. Mr. Alger, so far, hasn't given Julia Child any competition." Martin smiled.

"Or McDonald's," Jenny retorted, leaning her back against a tree, completely relaxed. Looking at Martin so calm and apparently carefree, she felt her inner tenseness ease. Not for the first time, she wondered how two brothers could be so totally different.

"A penny for your thoughts." Martin sat up.

"No thoughts. Just inhaling the peace, the beauty of this place."

"Shall we get started again?" Martin stood. "We can leave the basket here and pick it up on the way down."

"How much farther?"

"Believe it or not, about a five-minute walk. Funny, isn't it? We can't even see the cliffs from here and they're just over the rise. Hope we spot some Rocky Mountain sheep. Now they are majestic."

Martin seemed to really care about the land and the wildlife. He might not be exciting like Glenn, but at least he showed consideration. Glenn, with his contempt for amenities, crowded uninvited into her thoughts. How foolish she was to be concerned by a man whose vicissitudes of mood colored each encounter. But . . . she was going to remain neutral—so neutral that Switzerland would look like a warmonger.

Martin stopped and, motioning for her to come closer, pointed to the cliffs. "Take the binoculars and slowly sweep across those cliffs. The sheep are hard to spot. They blend right in with the bleached rock." Martin still stood close to her. With a half laugh he said, "Wish I had three hands—one to hold yours and two to remove the binoculars from around my neck." He stepped back to look at her. "You are lovely, you know." He bent his head and gently his lips touched hers, sweetly, tenderly.

The sun shone in the blue sky and a feeling of security eased through Jenny. The creaky old house with its mysterious, scraping sounds, the tense atmosphere when Glenn was around, the anxiety of Mrs. Hamilton—all faded from her thoughts as she basked in the safety of Martin's arms.

Then there was a rustling sound, and they stepped apart to see a ground squirrel scurry up a tree.

Martin laughed. "I guess we'd better search for those mountain sheep." He slipped the strap over his neck and handed her the binoculars.

Adjusting them, she scanned the cliffs. "I see something!" she called excitedly, yet managing to keep her voice low. "Fabulous! So rugged and still graceful. There are three of them. Here, look."

Martin aimed the glasses in the same direction. "Yes, three. You have good eyesight, Jenny. They're hard to spot with their coats blending in with the landscape. Sometimes I find them by looking for a dark spot against the stark white cliffs. Their curved horns and hoofs are brownish black.''

''Are we going to get closer?'' Jenny asked.

''No. It's still quite a hike up to those cliffs and those sheep would be gone, leaping to another ledge, before we got anywhere close. They're very skittish, and very surefooted.''

''It's a marvelous sight,'' she said. ''I feel privileged in seeing them. Thank you, Martin.''

''Thank you, Jenny,'' he returned solemnly. ''It's a pleasure to be able to show them to someone who really appreciates it. Now perhaps you understand why I need your help in making sure this island remains as is. Those sheep didn't come here by accident. They were brought here because, in our quest for more and more natural resources, we have destroyed much of their natural habitat and their numbers in the wild have dwindled alarmingly. This island was one of only a few areas left with a similar, but undisturbed habitat. So, a small herd was brought here in the hope that their numbers might increase.'' He paused for a moment, then added bitterly, ''And now Glenn wants to ruin it all with his plans for development.''

''Oh, no, Martin,'' said Jenny quickly. ''I'm sure that's not what Glenn wants. He wants a controlled development. That wouldn't hurt the sheep, surely, if it were properly planned.''

Martin gave a snort of derision. ''And how many controlled developments do you know that remain that way over the course of the years?'' he queried sarcastically.

Jenny sighed inwardly and gave up. Having seen the magnificent sight of the sheep, she could sympathize with Martin, but perversely, she could see Glenn's point, too. And having promised herself to remain neutral, here she was taking both sides! It was, she decided feelingly, an impossible situation.

''But enough of this,'' said Martin suddenly, perhaps sensing her thoughts. ''The tour isn't over yet. I want to show you the Eagles' Banquet Hall.'' They wandered down the hillside toward the picnic area. ''On our way home we'll swing around by the bridge and I'll show you the spot.''

It didn't seem as far back to the picnic area and the beach as it had going up. Jenny enjoyed the profusion of wildflowers growing in the meadows—Johnny-jump-ups, lupines, crocuses. ''I didn't realize we had climbed so high,'' she exclaimed.

''Yes, it's gradual for the most part, but still up.'' He helped her into the boat, shoved it away from the beach and climbed in. In a few minutes they were cruising across the lake, splitting the afternoon waves. Martin guided the boat toward the shore, then, shouting, he pointed to a creek. ''This is the lower creek that flows into Glacier Park. Salmon go up it around the second week of November to spawn and die. Eagles, both the bald and golden, around three hundred of them, congregate each year here and dive for salmon. There're a couple of bridges farther up where people watch. Quite a sight.''

"Martin, this has been such an exciting day. Thank you."

Martin smiled. "Being with someone who appreciates the beauty as I do has been my reward, Jenny." He turned the boat out toward the middle of the lake again and they followed the general shoreline. In the distance she could see Lone Lake Island. It seemed so far away.

Jenny sighed. It was difficult not to take sides, and she wished she had someone with whom she could share her concern over Mrs. Hamilton. But that wouldn't be fair, neither to Mrs. Hamilton herself nor to the nephews. She was an outsider, an employee, and none of it was any of her business. And she had never felt so alone.

They were closer to the shoreline now. Suddenly a large, black boat sped out from a cove, cutting in front of them.

Martin swore and swerved to miss it. "Damn fool. What does he think he's doing?" The boat cut in front of them again and this time Martin shut off his engine. The boat rocked from side to side in the wake of the black one. It circled around and came up alongside them. There were three Indians in it.

"Good afternoon. Do you have a boating permit for the use of our lake?" one of the Indians asked.

"Boating permit? Your lake? What are you talking about? We don't need a permit for this lake." Martin had his hand on the starter, ready to take off.

"This is our lake and ten feet up from the water edge is our land. For many years we let our resources be usurped by the whites. No longer. Now we expect to be paid for the use of our lake. Seven dollars and fifty cents for summer use only or twelve dollars for a year's permit.''

"You're crazy," exclaimed Martin in disgust. He turned the key and the motor caught.

"I wouldn't do that if I were you. Accidents do happen on this treacherous lake...'' the Indian spokesman said.

"Are you threatening me?" demanded Martin angrily. But he turned off the engine nevertheless.

"Now I have the decal, the boating permit,'' continued the Indian, unperturbed by Martin's outburst. "We'll sell you a permit and you can be on your way.''

"What if I don't have any money with me?''

"Then you'll sign this IOU and come to the tribal house in Risco tomorrow to settle up. Which will it be?'' The Indian waited. Not a muscle rippled and his expression was unreadable.

Would he really sink them or cause an accident? Jenny shivered, wishing she had her wallet. She'd be happy to pay the fee. The middle of a dark lake was no place to negotiate. She glanced at Martin. The tendons in his neck corded and his face was drawn.

"This is piracy. Blackmail. Illegal," he said.

"It's legal. Which will it be?''

"IOU." Martin shrugged. "Don't have my wallet with me.''

The Indian put a note with a pen clipped on it in a shallow basket tied to a pole and handed it over. "Sign. Keep the carbon. Put the carbon on the lower right side of your windshield. You'll get your decal after you pay tomorrow." He lowered the basket with Martin's signed IOU onto his deck and seconds later the black boat zoomed off.

"Those rabble-rousers," exclaimed Martin furiously. "If you hadn't been with me, Jenny, I'd have stood up to them. They have no claim to the land. But I couldn't take a chance with you." He taped the carbon to the windshield. "Most of this is Glenn's fault. He's really stirred up a hornet's nest by his land development schemes. Guess it's no wonder the Indians try to fight back, even if with outdated treaties." They drove back to the island in silence.

Jenny thanked Martin in the hallway again for the trip to see the mountain sheep. "A wonderful day." He headed for the library and she sat on the bottom step and removed her boots, then started up the stairs.

"Jenny. Jenny." Lone Willow stood at the bottom step. "Mrs. Hamilton would like you to go to her room as soon as you return."

"All right. Thanks, Lone Willow."

"Did you enjoy the tour? See any sheep?" the young woman asked.

"Yes. It was worth the hike. We saw three of them." She hurried up the stairs. Just before knocking at Mrs. Hamilton's door, she tucked in her shirt and smoothed her hair; then she rapped on the door and entered.

Mrs. Hamilton looked haggard, but greeted Jenny warmly. "Dear, thank you for coming. I've called Mr. Williams, my lawyer. He'll be here Saturday. Tomorrow I'd like you to help me sort some of Merci's

things. I know the answer to all of this is in her study."
She walked to the window and Jenny followed her.
The anguish in Mrs. Hamilton's voice was almost
frightening.

Mrs. Hamilton stood silently, a tortured lady, staring down at the lake below. It was choppy now, a
grayish lifeless color. From the window the lake
seemed to be right under her room.

Not looking at Jenny, Mrs. Hamilton reached for
her hand. "I'm frightened. I think I'm on to something, don't you know. Something very distressing.
Merci's journal. It changes everything...."

What could possibly be in Merci's journal that
could change everything, Jenny wondered. She shivered.

They both heard it. The squeak of a floorboard. It
sounded as if it were right outside the bedroom. Jenny
ran to the door and threw it open.

No one. The only sound was that of hurried footsteps going down the stairs.

CHAPTER EIGHT

CLOSING THE DOOR, Jenny deliberately assumed a cheerful face. "Nobody there, Mrs. Hamilton. My Aunt Blanche used to say that when her house creaked it was sighing." She laughed, hoping it would dispel the fear enveloping her.

Mrs. Hamilton shook her head. "No, my dear, this house wasn't sighing. Someone was eavesdropping, hoping to find out what I know." Her eyes filled with tears. "And all I know really is what is in Merci's journal concerning that lease agreement we found."

After reassuring Mrs. Hamilton that together they'd handle her worries, Jenny added, "Probably you're concerned over nothing—a document that later was rescinded or amended. We'll find the answer. Just wait and see."

DINNER THAT NIGHT was a disaster. Mrs. Hamilton had asked Lone Willow to share a tray with her in her bedroom, so only Glenn, Martin and Jenny were at the table. The cliché three's a crowd had never been more apt, and without doubt, Jenny was the third.

The disaster had begun in the library. When she walked into the library for cocktails, Glenn was at the tea cart bar. "Well, hello. How was your picnic?" he asked cheerfully. "See any Rocky Mountain sheep?"

"Three," Jenny replied, "and they were magnificent."

"Yes, quite a sight." He hesitated a moment, then walked around the tea cart and sat down beside her. "I . . . I always seem to be apologizing to you. One of these days I'm going to control my temper. What I'm trying to say is, I understand your position. Your duty is to Aunt Grace, and not to Martin or me."

Jenny gave an inner sigh of relief. At least she didn't have to do any explaining. She wondered whether Glenn realized how upset his aunt was. Probably not, since he hadn't been around much for the past twenty-four hours. Or had he? Had he been the one listening at his aunt's bedroom door this afternoon? Thoughts swirled in her head and a cold lump of fear settled in her stomach. She answered, "Thank you, Glenn, for understanding. Whatever is found belongs to Mrs. Hamilton. Besides, I don't know what you and Martin are looking for. Whatever . . . you can be sure I am not taking sides."

The words were no sooner out of her mouth than the door opened and Martin walked in. "Good evening," he said to the room at large, striding to Jenny's side and taking her hand in his, he added, "And how is my little nature lover this evening?" His tone indicated a special warmth, as though he knew he'd won a victory for her support.

Jenny was shocked, the more so since she'd just finished explaining her neutral stand to Glenn. What was wrong with Martin? Had he taken leave of his senses? Angrily she jerked her hand away and turned toward Glenn. There was no doubt in her mind what he was thinking. His dark eyes flashed ominously and his lips were drawn in a tight, narrow line. Even his nostrils seemed to flare in anger. But it was his face like a black thundercloud that haunted her as he stormed out of the room.

Martin shook his head. "I just don't understand that guy," he said in a nonchalant tone. "He's always uptight about something." He went to the bar. "May I fix you a drink?"

She whirled to face him. "Martin! How could you!" she exclaimed furiously. "You know as well as I do that I have no intention of being the punching bag between the two of you. God knows I've tried to explain it often enough. And now you—you..." Her anger overcame her ability to talk and she subsided into furious silence.

Martin moved toward her, a wry, contrite smile on his face. "I'm sorry, Jenny. I really didn't mean to offend you. But it was such a pleasant change to have someone who appreciated the island as I do with me this afternoon. And I honestly didn't expect Glenn to take it so seriously." Jenny turned away from him in disgust. For the second time, through no fault of her own, Glenn's trust in her had been shattered. And she had no idea how she was going to explain this one away.

A rumble of thunder announced the approach of a storm. At the same time Mr. Alger appeared to announce that dinner was served. Jenny hurried ahead of Martin into the dining room. Glenn stood behind his chair, awaiting their arrival. The tension in the room seemed to be building as much as the storm outside.

They sat down and self-consciously passed the serving dishes to one another. Finally Glenn asked, "Did you see any deer today, Jenny?" His voice was polite but distant.

"No, but on the way back Martin showed me where the eagles gather in the fall to catch fish. Fascinating." She tried to catch his eye, but he was looking just over her.

"Oh, the Eagles' Banquet. That's quite a sight."

"I'll tell you the real sight, Glenn," Martin interrupted. "Those Indians attacking us in the middle of the lake."

"Attacking you?" queried Glenn, and now he did turn to look at her. "What happened, Jenny?"

Trying to be completely unbiased, she stated the facts without coloring the picture with her fright. She finished with, "And so after Martin promised to pay, they sped away."

Glenn threw back his head and laughed.

"I don't think it was very funny, Glenn," she said stiffly. "Frankly, I was scared." She threw down her napkin and stood up. She'd had enough of Glenn for one evening. In her emotional state she found him unpredictable and self-centered. How could he think it funny when she'd been scared out of her wits?

"Hey, hey, Jenny." Glenn was at her side, his hand on her arm. "I'm not laughing at you or Martin. I'm sure it was a frightening experience. I'm laughing at the irony of it. We supposedly won the Indian wars and now they're assessing us to use the lake. Of course, there is a treaty giving ten feet from the lake's edge to the Indians, but no one pays any attention to it."

"Wrong, Glenn. They're paying attention now," she said.

A sudden rumble of thunder vibrated inside the house, rattling the cups on their saucers. Lightning flashed, and through the dining room window Jenny saw the black waves churning as if in discomfort.

"It was not a pleasant experience," observed Martin firmly. "I was worried about Jenny."

"They probably wouldn't have hurt her. They're just feeling their oats," said Glenn. "Recently they've won some land lawsuits in different parts of the country. Now, like children, they're pressing their advantages. It'll blow over." Glenn's dark eyes gleamed as though he were still amused by the encounter.

"Easy for you to say, Glenn. You weren't there. But as far as I'm concerned, their actions today show how uncivilized they are in spite of our efforts to educate them," retorted his brother callously.

A sudden gasp of anger sounded from the doorway. Jenny turned, and there stood Lone Willow on the threshold, her dark eyes glinting, her mouth taut. Lightning snapped across the sky, and the rain pelted at the windows.

Martin, too, saw her and half rose from his seat. "I . . . I didn't mean you, Ruthie," he stammered, obviously highly embarrassed.

"My name," said the young woman stiffly, "is Lone Willow. I am ashamed of my white name. Don't you ever call me 'Ruthie' again, Mr. Martin Larabie." She turned and was gone, the clacking sound of her quills fading as she moved down the hall.

"Lone Willow. Wait. Please wait." Jenny jumped up and hurried after her in dismay. She heard Glenn say, "You know, Martin, you really are a goddamn bigot."

"Glenn, you know I wouldn't do anything to hurt that girl." Martin's voice rose.

Jenny didn't catch up with Lone Willow. Although she called, the woman neither slowed her step nor answered. Jenny heard her bedroom door close firmly and walked on down the hall to her room. She knew she couldn't face an evening of sparring with Glenn and Martin.

Shutting her door, she undressed and got into bed to read. The storm was raging unabated now. The wind shook the house and it groaned in agony. A shutter banged. Rain pelted against the windows, setting up a drumming that seemed to reverberate around her room. When Jenny turned off the light, she found it difficult to go to sleep. The howling wind, the battering rain, the rumbling of thunder, followed by the crackling lightning, rattled the old house. She snuggled more firmly under the blankets. Every few minutes the room would light up for an instant. Even with

eyes squeezed closed she could see the lightning punc-
tuate the darkness.

She must have fallen asleep eventually, for about an
hour or so later she awoke with a start. She thought
she heard the clacking sound of porcupine quills. She
must be dreaming. Turning on the bedside light, she
looked at the clock—only 12:45. She flicked the light
off again, plumped up her pillow and huddled once
more under the covers. The rain was steady now and
the wind had quieted. A good sleeping night, she
thought, wide-awake. Images flashed through her
mind. Papers scattered over a library floor, Algers
threatening countenance, Mrs. Hamilton's anguished
face as she held a journal close to her chest, a yellowed deed paper signed by Gray Wolf, Martin with
his easygoing manners, an image of Glenn, dark and
forbidding, followed almost immediately by a vision
of his handsome face open and friendly, his dark eyes
lit with pleasure and the joy of life.

Glenn's image faded, and a picture of the black boat
and the three Indians flashed across her thought
screen. She shivered. She felt herself tightening and
that old sleep-delayer game, what if, began its series.
What if Martin had tried to make a run for it? What
if the Indians had swamped their boat? And, ridiculously, what if they had taken her hostage until Martin paid for the permit? What if . . . At this rate she'd
never get to sleep.

Then she heard the familiar scraping noise coming
from Merci's old study. She lay still, listening. There

was a sound of something falling, a stack of books or boxes, a kind of *thud* followed by a muffled curse.

She jumped out of bed and grabbed her robe. No doubt about it now. There was definitely someone in that room. She didn't care if Lone Willow liked it or not, but she was going to her room to get her. Carefully she unlocked her door and turned the doorknob. The hall was dimly lit and she hurried around the railing to Lone Willow's room at the head of the stairs. She rapped softly, then more firmly. Finally she whispered, "Lone Willow. Open up. It's Jenny." There was no answer. She turned the doorknob and peeked in. The bedside lamp was on, but Lone Willow wasn't there.

Jenny's heart pounded and her legs felt suddenly shaky. Someone was in Merci's study. She'd heard him curse. Him? Maybe it had been a "her"! Lone Willow wasn't in her room. Before she could weigh the pros and cons, Jenny headed down the stairs to Glenn's room. She didn't care if he was angry with her or even laughed at her. She just wanted someone, anyone, to take the burden of her fear. Glenn's door was closed. She knocked and called his name, but there was no answer. She opened the door and switched on the light. His bed was untouched.

By now she was feeling a little foolish. She could think of reasons why she thought she heard someone in the locked study. At night sounds are sometimes distorted, she reasoned. The thud could have been someone in another part of the house dropping something. The clacking sound of the porcupine quills could have been Lone Willow in a different part of the house.

Nevertheless she continued down the hall to Martin's room. She raised her hand to rap on the door, but saw it was partly open. She called his name, then reached in and turned on the light. Another empty room greeted her gaze.

All the way back to the third floor she had an inane desire to laugh, hysterically, she realized. Now she just wanted to get to her room and lock the door. Her mouth was dry and icy beads of perspiration wet her forehead. Where on earth could everyone be? And why were they all up in the middle of the night? For one ridiculous moment, she wondered if they were all in the virgin's bedroom. But that still didn't explain how they might have gotten there.

She passed Lone Willow's room and the bathroom, but as she started past the door leading to the fourth floor ballroom, she noticed the door was ajar. Quietly she edged it open, expecting to look up into blackness. She almost cried out when a light, as though from a flashlight, swept across the upper part of the steps. Her first impulse was to slam the door and race for her room. But then she thought it might be Mrs. Hamilton, looking for something, and perhaps she could help her.

Gathering her long robe in one hand, Jenny gripped the banister with the other and started up the narrow passageway to the ballroom. There was a musty disused smell to the whole area. She thought of spiders spinning their webs and waiting for their victim. Stepping on the very edge of the steps so that they wouldn't creak, she slowly edged up the stairs. Her bare feet felt like blocks of ice. Her heart pounded so hard she thought she could hear it. The silence in the black abyss ahead of her was like a magnet drawing her closer and closer to the top. Should she call out so as not to startle Mrs. Hamilton? But maybe it wasn't Mrs. Hamilton. Maybe it had just been a flash of lightning she'd seen.

She was in the doorway of the ballroom now. Her eyes seemed to be adjusting to the darkness. She could see the outline of the piano and the chairs along one of the walls; the door to the cloakroom was directly opposite from where she stood.

Taking a deep breath, she glanced around the room again. Now she felt hot and her gown beneath her robe clung. Lightning flashed, highlighting parts of the room, and in that instant she saw someone lolling against the cloakroom doorframe. And it certainly wasn't Mrs. Hamilton. A chill raced down Jenny's spine. She gasped and turned to run down the stairs. Before she could feel for the banister, she sensed someone behind her. Then the smell—pungent, onionlike. A sharp pain exploded in her head. She felt the push at the small of her back. And she was falling.

CHAPTER NINE

"JENNY. JENNY. Wake up. Come on now. Be a good girl. Open your eyes."

It was Glenn's voice. She wanted to wake up. Why was he so far away?

"She's stirring. I think she's coming around, Aunt Grace."

Now someone was rubbing and patting her hands.

"Do we dare move her? She might catch cold lying here in the drafty hallway, don't you know. I'll get a blanket."

Jenny heard the clicking of Mrs. Hamilton's heels. What was she doing up here on the third floor? Opening her eyes, she saw Glenn sitting beside her. But why was she on the floor? Had she fainted?

"Thank God you're awake," exclaimed Glenn fervently. "Did you trip? What were you doing on the ballroom stairs?"

Jenny closed her eyes again, trying to sort out her muddled thoughts. She was surprised at the concern in Glenn's voice. Wasn't he angry with her? Or had he apologized again? She couldn't keep track of his feelings. Her head hurt. Maybe she was dreaming and soon she'd wake up.

"Jenny's conscious, Aunt Grace," she heard him call out.

"Oh, my head," she groaned. From the recesses of her mind a picture emerged. She saw herself seeing the ballroom shrouded in shadows and the crackling lightning showing the figure in the doorway of the cloakroom. She shivered, remembering the feeling of someone behind her—the pungent smell of onions—the terror as she turned to dash down the stairs. "Who pushed me?"

"Pushed you!" exclaimed Glenn. "There was no one on the stairway, just you at the bottom in a heap. I was just coming up to go to bed, when I heard a bumping down the steps. When I reached the third floor, there you were sprawled at the foot of the ball-room stairs." Gently, Glenn pushed the hair back from her face and looked into her eyes. "Can you follow my finger?" he asked.

She focused on his finger as he moved it from one side of her range of vision to the other.

"Good. Don't think you have a concussion," he said.

"Oh, dear Jenny, what a terrible thing to happen. Do you think you can walk to your bedroom if Glenn helps you?" Holding a blanket, Mrs. Hamilton stood over her. "I'm so glad you're conscious. You looked so pale and vulnerable lying there, don't you know. Here, Glenn, you take one arm and I'll hold the other."

"I can carry her, Aunt Grace." Glenn stood up and then crouched to scoop her up in his arms with no apparent effort. "Can you put your arms around my neck, Jenny?"

Obediently she did as she was told, but couldn't help wondering if she was putting her arms around someone who, moments before, had pushed her.

Mrs. Hamilton ran ahead. "Whatever made you go up those steep stairs, child, and in the dark? Were you sleepwalking?" She fluffed up the pillow and stepped aside for Glenn to lay her on the bed, then spread the blanket over her. "Do you hurt anywhere? I see the bruise on your forehead. Oh, I wish Lone Willow would come. She's so good when I ail, don't you know." She patted the blanket. "Do your arms and legs work?"

"I think so." Jenny touched the back of her head and felt the matted blood. "I think my head is bleeding, though. Someone hit me."

"You hit it on the steps coming down, Jenny. There was no one on the steps and I was there almost immediately after you hit bottom," Glenn said firmly.

Even to her aching head, Glenn's explanation sounded pat, but the sound of clacking porcupine quills interrupted that train of thought. Lone Willow appeared in the doorway. "Is Jenny sick?" she asked, unbuttoning her heavy sweater.

"She's had a bad fall, Lone Willow. Glad you're home. Would you get a cloth and some water? We'll clean up that cut." Glenn gently turned Jenny's head to the side to look at the wound. His long, graceful fingers probed tenderly around the wound. "Hey, you really did get banged up. Don't think you need stitches, but it's quite a gash."

In a few minutes Lone Willow was back with wash-cloth, towels and methiolate. "Mrs. Hamilton, you look so tired." Lone Willow sponged the laceration. "I'll take care of Jenny. You go on to bed."

"Well, if you're sure you don't need me..." Mrs. Hamilton started for the door and then came back to the side of the bed. Leaning over, she kissed Jenny on the cheek. "For such a slip of a girl, you certainly made a lot of noise falling down those steps. I'm thankful nothing seems to be broken. Sleep in tomorrow, dear. Good night."

When Lone Willow finished cleaning her up, she painted methiolate on the various cuts on her arms, legs and face. "You look like one of us now, Jenny," she said with a laugh.

"And what more could you ask?" Glenn's voice was warm with affection and his eyes lit up as he smiled at Lone Willow.

Jenny let them talk, while thoughts whirled in her head. It was long past Mrs. Hamilton's bedtime, so why was she still in her high heels? And how convenient that Glenn had just happened to be coming up stairs for bed when she was coming down! Lone Willow hadn't been in her room, either. Had she been in the ballroom? And Martin?

"Where's Martin?" Jenny asked, and sensed a sudden stiffening in Glenn.

"I saw him in the library just before I came up the stairs," Lone Willow said. "There. You're painted up fit for a war dance." She picked up the basin of water. "Now don't look at yourself, Jenny. It'll scare you. I'll be back to tuck you in for the night—or for what's left of it, anyway." She hurried from the room.

Jenny lay still, not looking at Glenn. She never felt more like an orphan in her life. Aching in her loneliness, she felt the tears gathering for the rush down her cheek.

Then she heard Glenn's voice, soft and gentle. "Jenny, thank God, you're all right." He leaned over and kissed her forehead as if she were a hurt child.

No onion smell, she noted almost subconsciously. Just a clean masculine odor with a slight hint of a spicy cologne. Could that dispel an onion smell? No, nothing, not even fancy cologne, could dispel that odor. Jenny badly wanted to tell him how frightened she was and how alone she felt.... But could she trust him? She wasn't sure.

She turned her head and looked at him. "Glenn, I *was* pushed," she insisted. "And whoever it was hit me over the head first."

He straightened. "I know," he agreed surprisingly. "There's no other way you could have got that gash. But I didn't want Aunt Grace to know." Taking her hand in his, he paused for a moment, hesitating before adding, "Jenny, I think you should pack up and leave this place. You're in danger."

"Leave?" Jerking her hand from his, she sat up in bed, and immediately wished she hadn't as the pain exploded in her head once more. Why was he suddenly so concerned for her welfare? Was there something in the historical papers he didn't want her to find? Maybe he felt she was getting close to discovering something that would put Martin in Mrs. Hamilton's favor.

"Well, will you?" he persisted.

"No way, Glenn Larabie," she replied firmly. "I was hired for the summer to help Mrs. Hamilton. I need this job. The historical papers are necessary for my thesis." She winced as a particularly vicious stab of pain shot through her head. Glenn put his hands on her shoulders and eased her back to the pillow. "Who'd want to hurt me, anyway?" she added weakly. "I don't know anything."

"Well, someone thinks you do," he remarked grimly. "Whoever hit you on the head and shoved you down the stairs wasn't joking. It was a warning." Abruptly he stood and began pacing about the room. "I don't know what the hell is going on." His voice softened. "I just know I don't want anything to happen to you. I care about you...."

Jenny felt utterly confused. This couldn't be the same Glenn. Either that or she was dreaming. Or—oh, horrible thought—was he comforting her simply to get information and moments later would return to his distant, cool self? Much as she might want to tell him everything—the finding of the lease, Merci's journal and his aunt's distress—something, some glimmer of suspicion, held her back. *Someone* had pushed her down those ballroom stairs and that someone could have been Glenn.

He stopped his pacing and returned to her bedside. "Tell me everything you did from the time you returned from the picnic—who you saw and talked with," he commanded, sitting at the foot of her bed.

"Let's see." Jenny stalled for time, trying to sort out what she'd tell and what she'd keep to herself. "Lone Willow told me Mrs. Hamilton wanted to see me, so before I even changed I went to her room."

"What did Aunt Grace want?"

"Oh, nothing in particular. We talked about tomorrow's work plan. You know, which box of papers to sort next...."

A look of disbelief crossed Glenn's face. Obviously she hadn't fooled him with her vague answer.

Embarrassed that he had caught her deliberate evasiveness so easily, she fought to keep her voice steady. "While I was with Mrs. Hamilton, we heard a noise. Someone was eavesdropping at her bedroom door. But when I opened it, all I heard was footsteps hurrying down the main stairs. I saw no one."

"Whoever was listening at the door probably pushed you down the stairs," Glenn muttered, more to himself than to her. He was silent a moment, then asked, "Why were you in the ballroom?"

Jenny didn't tell him about the noise coming from his mother's old study, but explained she had been worried about Lone Willow after Martin's comments in the dining room and had gone to her room to talk with her. Lone Willow hadn't been in her room, but when Jenny had passed the door to the ballroom, it had been open and she'd seen light flicking from above. She thought it might have been Mrs. Hamilton and she'd gone upstairs to the ballroom to see if she'd needed help.

Glenn was silent for a moment. "Is that everything?"

With fingers crossed beneath the blankets, Jenny nodded briefly. She wasn't ready to trust him completely yet. And besides, her head throbbed too much to go into further details now.

"Ready for me to tuck you in, Jenny?" Lone Willow, dressed in her bathrobe, stood in the doorway. "I'll be glad to get a blanket and sit beside you tonight if you're nervous."

"No, thanks, Lone Willow. I'm sure I'll be all right. The storm's over and I'm beginning to feel relaxed and sleepy. Silly for you to lose sleep watching me sleep."

"Good night, Jenny." Glenn reached out and patted her hand. "Glad you weren't hurt too seriously. See you in the morning." Nodding to Lone Willow, he left the room.

Lone Willow turned off the light. "I'll leave our doors open, Jenny. If you call, I'll hear you. I'm a light sleeper. Good night."

Jenny turned over on her side and closed her eyes. She felt as if she were in a labyrinth and each turn took her deeper into the maze. She wished she could trust someone. Even though Glenn said he cared, Jenny wondered. Gingerly she turned over to her other side. Would she ever get to sleep?

The numbers on her luminous clock showed almost two. She was thirsty. The light from Lone Willow's room brightened hers. No need to call Lone Willow. Holding on to the edge of the bed, Jenny tested her equilibrium, then walked cautiously to the bathroom. Returning, she could hear the murmur of low voices. Who was Lone Willow talking to? Jenny edged down the hall past the closed door of the small bedroom to the young woman's open door. Sitting on the side of the bed with his back to the door was Glenn, holding Lone Willow in his arms. One hand stroked Lone Willow's long black hair. Softly he said, "So dear to me. You know I love you."

Jenny's heart sank. So much for the depth of Glenn's feelings for her. Leaning against the hall wall, Jenny managed to get back to her room. Once in bed, she shivered, the cold coming from within her. She wouldn't be taken in by him again, no matter how many apologies he made. How glad she was now that she hadn't trusted him and told him everything she knew.

LONE WILLOW WOKE HER at eight. "How do you feel?" she asked. "Does your head still hurt? Are you stiff?" She set the tray with coffee, juice, toast, eggs and bacon on the bedside table. "No need to hurry, Jenny, but your breakfast is hot. Don't let it get too cold. Need help getting to the bathroom?"

Gingerly Jenny stood, expecting to be light-headed, but the room stayed in focus, and except for some stiffness and soreness, she felt fine.

After brushing her teeth, she splashed cool water on her face. Last night seemed like a bad dream. First the definitive noise and voiced curse coming from Merci's study, then her frantic search for someone—Lone Willow, Glenn, or Martin—to no avail, the trip to the ballroom, the smell of onions and her fall. She remembered Glenn and his tender concern. Had he really said, "I care about you"? Then how could he have said "I love you" to Lone Willow? The whole sequence of events must be a nightmare. Picking up her brush, she started to brush her hair, but stopped in a hurry. The lump on her head, at least, was no dream.

She had just finished the breakfast tray, when Martin rapped at the open door. "Good morning, Jenny. May I come in?" He pulled a chair up beside the bed. "What's this about your falling down the stairs? Aunt Grace told me you were lucky not to have any broken bones."

"Just a couple of cuts and a bruised pride is all, Martin."

"What were you doing on those stairs, anyway?"

She hesitated before replying. Should she tell him what she'd told Glenn? Martin hadn't been in his room last night, either, she reminded herself. And for all his easygoing manner and outward charm, she was no more certain she could trust him than anyone else.

She remembered Mrs. Hamilton's rationalization and used it. "I must have been sleepwalking," she replied. "The storm made me uneasy. I feel like a naughty child who wouldn't stay in bed." She laughed, trying to make light of her supposed sleepwalking.

"The storms in this area are fierce and can be frightening if you haven't been through a few," agreed Martin, apparently believing her explanation. "I'm happy you weren't seriously hurt. You look surprisingly rested this morning, all things considered." He reached out and patted her hand, then reached up to her head. His fingers gently touched the bruise on her forehead. "That looks nasty."

"It feels better this morning than it did last night," she told him absently, her mind intent on another train of thought. Could it have been this man who had pushed her down those stairs? He also could well have had the opportunity. She was about to ask him whether he'd been in the library all evening, when they were interrupted by a sound from the doorway.

Lone Willow stood at the entrance to Jenny's room. "Finished with your tray, Jenny?" she asked as she came in. She nodded briefly at Martin. "Good morning." Obviously she was still angry with him, and Jenny could hardly blame her.

Martin jumped to his feet. "Ruthie—Lone Willow—please forgive me for my stupid remark last night. I was angry at being accosted in the middle of the lake and concerned for Jenny's safety. It was unkind of me, I know, and totally uncalled for. You know I'm usually critical of those who generalize, but last night my anger got the better of me. I know it and I apologize."

Lone Willow made no comment.

"Please say you'll forgive me," he asked softly, wistfully.

Lone Willow looked down. "It's all right, Martin. I'll try to understand," she replied quietly.

Martin crossed the room quickly and gathered her to him. "My dear Lone Willow, I don't think of you as a citizen—Indian or American—but as my sister."

The tension in Jenny's bedroom lightened with this reconciliation. With Lone Willow sitting at the foot of her bed and Martin in a chair beside it, the three of them rehashed last night's accident.

"I'm glad the sound didn't carry to the library," Martin remarked fervently. "Glenn is much more levelheaded in an emergency than I am."

"Wasn't Glenn with you in the library?" Jenny asked.

"No, I was there all evening, reading. I don't know where he was."

Well, that was two questions answered, thought Jenny. Martin was accounted for, but where had Glenn been? In the ballroom? Jenny was doubly glad she hadn't told him everything she knew.

Lone Willow spoke up. "Mrs. Hamilton and I had just returned from Bobby Black Bear's. We walked over after dinner—in between storms. Mrs. Hamilton wanted some fresh air. We stayed until the rain let up."

Jenny remembered the sound of Mrs. Hamilton's heels as the woman had gone to get the blanket to cover her. "Did Mrs. Hamilton walk to Bobby Black Bear's in high heels?" she queried.

Lone Willow laughed. "No. She keeps a pair of loafers by the back porch. She slips them on when she goes walking about the island. That's why she reached you before me. I was cleaning the mud off her shoes for her."

"What does Mr. Alger do with his evenings?" Jenny asked.

"Television. Loud television," Martin growled.

Lone Willow laughed. "He does play it loud," she agreed. "I think he turns it on as soon as he gets to his room regardless of the program." She stood. "I'd better get to work." She lifted the tray from the bed. "Mrs. Hamilton said for you to 'lie a-bed' and rest."

Martin followed Lone Willow out of the room and down the stairs.

Jenny lay quietly for a moment, but her thoughts would not be laid to rest. She wondered if Mr. Alger's loud television wasn't a ruse—a means of covering up his real activities, such as snooping around in the library or pushing a secretary down the ballroom steps. Certainly, as far as she was concerned, he was an unpleasant enough person to be capable of such actions. But what possible motive could he have?

This is ridiculous, she told herself sternly. Throwing the covers back, she headed for the closet. It would be better for her to be working than worrying about who had pushed her down those steps and why.

CHAPTER TEN

IT WAS AFTER NINE when she walked into the library to begin work. Mrs. Hamilton was at the desk and papers were scattered all about. Merci's journal was in her lap.

"Good morning, Mrs. Hamilton."

"Jenny, dear. I didn't expect you to get up today. Are you all right?" Laying the journal on the desk, she hurried to Jenny. Putting her arm around her shoulder, she led her to a chair. "Perhaps you should just take it easy today."

"No, I'm all right, really, Mrs. Hamilton. I'm anxious to help you. It'll take my mind off a bruise here and there."

"If you get tired, say so. I do appreciate your help, don't you know." She returned to her chair, put the journal back in her lap and began flipping through different papers on her desk.

Jenny moved the chair to the file cabinet and once again started filing the papers from the box. This was the last box and then everything would be in order, except for Merci's things stored in her old study. They worked without talking for over an hour. The only sound was the clock chiming the half-hours and, periodically, Mrs. Hamilton's sighing, as though she were resigned to some unknown fate.

"That finishes the last box, Mrs. Hamilton. Now what would you like me to do?"

"My goodness, you're quick. I thought this was going to take all summer, don't you know?" Mrs. Hamilton laughed. "It certainly would have with those other secretaries, or if I'd had to do it myself." She leaned back in her chair. "Let's take a break. I'll ring for Lone Willow to bring us some coffee, and then we'll go to Merci's study. There's still a lot to sort up there." She jingled the silver bell on her desk. In a few minutes Lone Willow appeared.

"Ready for coffee so soon, Mrs. Hamilton?" She glanced at her wristwatch. "Unless I'm running slow, it's only ten-fifteen."

"We're running fast. And bother with the schedule! Let's have coffee now, Lone Willow."

In a few minutes they were grouped around the low table, drinking coffee and eating doughnut holes.

"Jenny, I've been thinking about last night, and I believe—" Mrs. Hamilton's finger twirled the lock of hair rapidly "—you must have gotten overly tired on your hike with Martin. And then that fierce storm. So then you just walked in your sleep, don't you know." She dabbed her mouth with a napkin. "There. That settles that."

Jenny didn't know whether her "there" settled the coffee break or the mystery of her falling down the ballroom stairs.

"It was lucky Glenn heard you when you fell," observed Lone Willow, putting the cups and saucers on the tray.

"Goodness me, for such a slight girl you make a lot of noise, Jenny." Mrs. Hamilton stood. "Time to go back to work. Thank you, Lone Willow for the coffee. If you need us, Jenny and I will be working in Merci's study."

Jenny followed Mrs. Hamilton into her bedroom to the door leading into the study. Mrs. Hamilton carried Merci's journal under her arm. Taking a black key from a ring, she fitted it in the key hole and with a slight push opened the door.

Jenny had been so curious about that room she could hardly wait to finally see it. But what a nondescript room! There was a leather rocking chair and an end table, and bookshelves had been built along one wall. A black marble fireplace, identical to the one in her room, shared a common wall with hers. The most interesting part of the room was the tower. It rounded one corner out by at least five feet and the uncurtained windows went almost from ceiling to floor. Looking down on the lake below, Jenny realized that the tower actually hung out over the water at this point. The lake was choppy and gray today, as though the storm had churned up the bottom.

"It's a spectacular sight, isn't it?" observed Mrs. Hamilton. "Well, let's get started. I don't think we'll come upon anything more for the files downstairs. Just clippings and Merci's letters and personal effects." She hesitated, looking down at Merci's jour-

nal on the maple desk. "It's all in here." She tapped
the journal. "I have proof of something I've suspected a long time. This evening, Jenny, I will meet
with the boys at five-thirty before cocktails and discuss this matter with them. Then we can proceed with
definite plans."

Mrs. Hamilton was right. Merci's study held no new
surprises or disclosures. Jenny was itching with curiosity as to what Mrs. Hamilton had discovered in the
journal. Had she found a bill of sale to go with the
lease of the island to Grandfather Clayborn? Jenny
longed to know but refrained from asking. It was
really none of her business and only right that the
family know first.

Quickly they sorted through four or five boxes of
newspaper clippings and personal letters. There were
no deeds or wills or treaties among her things. Mrs.
Hamilton sat at the maple desk, rereading Merci's
journal, while Jenny sat on the rug with piles of clippings in front of her.

"Let's call it a day, Jenny," said Mrs. Hamilton finally. "I know it's early, but I'm tired." She stood
and, rotating her shoulders, sighed. "I guess if I'd sit
up straight, I wouldn't get so weary at the desk."

Jenny followed Mrs. Hamilton, with Merci's journal under her arm, out of the room and watched as she
again took the long, black key from her ring and
locked the door, testing it to be sure it was secure. "No
need for you to come downstairs with me, Jenny. You
rest until lunch. I'm going to have my lunch in my
room, so I'll see you at six for cocktails." She lin-

gered at the bedroom door. Then, laying her hand on Jenny's arm, she squeezed. "You've been wonderful help, Jenny, so patient and cheerful and eager to please. Your parents would have been very proud of you."

"Thank you, Mrs. Hamilton."

"I can see the end of the tunnel finally. Tonight after I've talked with the boys, we can make plans on when and how to present the papers to the historical society. That's important, my dear, and we have lots of work to do getting the documents ready. When Wilbur Williams comes on Saturday, I can make arrangements for the disposition of this island. All legal and final." She started down the hallway, then stopped. "Thank you again, Jenny. You've been a wonderful help. See you this evening, dear."

Glenn, Martin, Lone Willow and Jenny had lunch together. For once it was a quiet, civilized meal. Her accident, as Martin called it, was briefly mentioned and then the conversation turned to baseball.

"What are your plans for the afternoon, Lone Willow?" Glenn asked toward the end of the meal.

"No more procrastinating for me," she replied with a laugh. "I'm spending the afternoon with the history books. I promised Mrs. Hamilton that I'd get to it."

"I'm taking Alger to town for some groceries. Want to ride along, Jenny?" Martin asked.

"No, thanks. I'm going to take a short walk and then read."

"I'll come with you, Jenny," Glenn said, then added, "if it's all right with you."

"Sure." She answered in as composed and unemotional a voice as his. Excusing herself, she went to her room for a sweater.

Ten minutes later she and Glenn were walking along the path leading to Bobby Black Bear's. Glenn seemed ill at ease. Surely he wasn't suffering from a guilty conscience, she thought sarcastically. Finally he said, "I'm glad you're all right, Jenny. I worry about you."

"No need to," she replied coolly. "I'm blessed with a hard head."

Glenn laughed, then asked how the work was going.

She told him that Mrs. Hamilton had taken her to Merci's to sort out his mother's letters and newspaper clippings. She thought he would ask if they had found anything important, but, to her surprise, he didn't. Instead he talked about college and the classes he had enjoyed and how pleased he was that Lone Willow was doing her correspondence course.

When they reached Shadow Shallows, Bobby Black Bear was hoeing in his garden. He looked up and let out a yell. "Hey, great you two stopped by. Come on in and have some iced tea."

They followed him up the steps to the back porch. Suddenly she had the same feeling she'd had in the ballroom the previous night, just before she had been hit on the head. But no one was behind her now, she knew. And the day was bright and sunny, not dark and stormy as it had been then. Then she knew. It was the smell. The smell of onions. Lying on a narrow table were a half-dozen braided onions drying in the sun. She looked at Bobby Black Bear holding the kitchen door ajar for them, his open smiling face and dark honest eyes. It couldn't have been him, she thought. Why would he want to push her down the stairs? Come to think of it, why would *anyone* want to push her down the stairs?

"Are you all right, Jenny?" Glenn asked. "You look drawn. The walk wasn't too far for you, was it?"

"I'm all right. Iced tea will taste good."

Glenn told Bobby Black Bear about her fall. "And someone pushed her, BB," he concluded.

"Pushed her?" exclaimed the young man. "Who? And more important, why?"

"Don't know, BB," replied Glenn solemnly, then paused before adding, "tonight Aunt Grace wants to talk with Martin and me, so I guess she's made up her mind about the disposition of the island."

"Is that what Mrs. Hamilton wants to talk about? She sent word via Lone Willow this morning that she wanted me at your place at five-thirty tonight." Bobby Black Bear poured more iced tea for them. "She must have something else on her mind, too, otherwise she wouldn't have invited me."

Both Bobby Black Bear and Glenn laughed.

"You know Aunt Grace, BB." Glenn looked over at Jenny. "We've got to go. Jenny is looking limp. Think she'd better hit the sack for a few hours."

The walk home was quick and silent. Glenn seemed miles away. When they reached the house, he asked,

"Want me to walk you up the stairs, or do you think you can make it?"

"I'm fine, Glenn. Thanks for going for a walk with me." She turned quickly and headed up the stairs. She passed Lone Willow's room and could hear her typing. As she walked by the closed door leading up to the ballroom, she stopped and quietly turned the knob. Opening the door, she looked up the narrow stairway. Even in daytime the light wasn't bright, but at least she could see the steps. Without stopping to think, she was on her way up those stairs. She had to see the ballroom in daylight, recreate the images, review her feelings of last night.

She stood at the entry. In daylight the ballroom looked just as it was, a dusty, forgotten room. The piano with its covered keys, the chairs lined up along one wall, the light fixtures with their light bulbs missing, even the floor, a parquet, all lacked luster and life. There was nothing here but memories of a glorious past. Then she saw something lying by the stair railing. A porcupine quill! It had been attached to a necklace, a necklace like Lone Willow's. Jenny clutched it in her fist. Her head throbbed and now her legs felt shaky. Lone Willow couldn't have done it. She was sweet and kind. And besides, she'd been out with Mrs. Hamilton.

Jenny's head pounded with accusations, explanations, suspicions, rationalizations. She was suddenly tired and completely discouraged. Holding on to the stair railing, she crept down the steps to her room. Locking the door, she went to her dresser and buried the porcupine quill underneath her sweaters. Demons of doubt pricked her thoughts as she lay on the bed, trying to relax and rest. Over and over she reviewed the events, the people, her feelings. Finally she dozed off into an uneasy slumber. The knocking on the door seemed to be part of a bad dream. Rousing herself, she called out, "Who's there?"

"Lone Willow. Open up, please."

Jenny climbed out of bed and unlocked the door. "What time is it?"

"Almost six and..." Lone Willow's voice trembled. "We can't find Mrs. Hamilton. She told Bobby Black Bear, Glenn and Martin to meet her at five-thirty in the library, but she didn't show up."

"I'll dress," said Jenny quickly. "Mrs. Hamilton probably took a walk." Even as she said it she knew it couldn't be. Mrs. Hamilton miss a time schedule? Impossible!

Jenny and Lone Willow joined Glenn, Martin and Bobby Black Bear in the library.

"You've checked her room, Lone Willow, and the bathroom?" Glenn asked.

"Yes. I even looked in her closet and under the bed." Lone Willow stood by Bobby Black Bear. He reached for her hand.

"Let's not panic," suggested Martin, surprisingly languidly. "Aunt Grace has to be somewhere on the island. Both boats are at the dock." He poured himself a drink. "I suggest we fan out. Someone go to the fourth floor, someone to the third, and then we'll meet here in the library. Hopefully with Aunt Grace."

"Fine, Martin. Incidentally, has anyone asked Mr. Alger about Aunt Grace? Maybe she told him something." Glenn shook his head at Martin's invitation for a drink.

"Right. You want to do that, Glenn?" Martin asked. "I'll go to the ballroom and you two girls look on the second and third floors. BB, you check the main floor and immediately outside the house."

It was some time later when they all reassembled in the library. No one had a clue to Mrs. Hamilton's whereabouts. She had simply vanished.

"What did Mr. Alger say?" Martin asked, mixing yet another drink. "Had he seen Aunt Grace this afternoon?"

"He said that he fixed iced tea for Lone Willow to take up to Aunt Grace about three this afternoon. Otherwise he doesn't know anything." Glenn shook his head. "That guy...."

"So you saw Aunt Grace this afternoon?" Martin whirled around from the tea cart and confronted Lone Willow.

"Hey, Martin, this isn't Perry Mason. Lighten up." Glenn's tone was conciliatory, but firm. "How about your place, BB? Think she might have gone to meet you and fell or something?" Glenn asked.

It was still light outside and Bobby Black Bear offered to check the path leading to his house.

"Dinner's ready," Mr. Alger announced from the doorway. "Is anyone going to eat, or what do you want done with the food?"

"Put the salads back in the refrigerator, please, Mr. Alger." Lone Willow spoke up. "Later I'll warm up our supper."

Mr. Alger just stood there, and then, turning to Martin, asked, "Is that what I should do, huh?"

Glenn stepped forward. "You heard Lone Willow, Alger," he snapped. "That'll be all."

Mr. Alger shrugged and turned away. His shuffling step seemed as disrespectful and sneering as his shrug.

"I'll hurry on to my house. Be back as soon as possible." With a reassuring pat on Lone Willow's arm, Bobby Black Bear headed for the door.

Martin was at Mrs. Hamilton's desk now, opening and closing drawers.

"What are you looking for?" Glenn asked.

"Mother's journal. I don't see it anywhere. Do you know where it is, Jenny?"

"The last time I saw it Mrs. Hamilton had it tucked under her arm."

Again Lone Willow and Jenny climbed the stairs, this time to search for the journal in Mrs. Hamilton's room. But it, too, had vanished.

It was dark by the time Bobby Black Bear returned. "Ran all the way," he said breathlessly. "Thought I'd come upon her at any moment. Coming back, searched along the side of the path, too. Called for her, but nothing." Bobby Black Bear sat down on the couch, his breathing shallow and jerky. "Glenn, do you think we should call for help from the mainland? Maybe the sheriff?"

"We were working in Merci's study," Jenny said. "Perhaps she's there and has forgotten the time."

"Aunt Grace forget the time!" Martin laughed. "Her whole life was a time schedule." He turned back to the tea cart and poured another drink. "A time to eat and a time to drink and . . ."

And a time to die. The words from the Bible rushed into Jenny's mind, chilling her.

"Nevertheless I think we should look," said Glenn.

"Who has the key to Mother's study?" Martin asked. "Not that we'll need it if Aunt Grace is there."

"Mrs. Hamilton had it. It's a big black iron one. It was on her brass ring." Hurrying to the desk, Jenny, glad to have something concrete to do, searched for the key ring. She knew Mrs. Hamilton couldn't be in the study. No one had gone through her bedroom. "It's not here," she told the assembled company after a few minutes of fruitless searching.

"Maybe we can pick the lock." Glenn headed for the doorway and then stopped. "If Jenny doesn't mind our invading her bedroom."

"No, please see if Mrs. Hamilton is in the . . . adjoining room," she finished weakly. "Virgin's bedroom" sounded so brash, almost disrespectful to the dead. But she didn't know that Mrs. Hamilton was dead! Why did she think she was? Was it because Martin talked of her in the past, saying her whole life had been a time schedule? And come to think of it, why had he used the past tense?

Pulling herself together, she followed the searchers upstairs. At the door leading into Merci's study, Glenn took his key ring out to see if any of his keys would unlock the door. Finally, turning to Jenny, he asked if she had a manicure stick. "You know. The thing you wrap cotton on."

"An orange stick." Lone Willow and Jenny answered in unison. Jenny went to the bathroom drawer for her manicure set. Although Glenn seemed to know what he was doing with the wooden instrument, it wouldn't unlock the door.

"I'll get a screwdriver and hammer," offered Bobby Black Bear, hurrying from the room. In a few minutes he returned with the tools, and a few pounds later the lock was broken.

Jenny stood back, almost afraid to look in the room, but Martin, shoving ahead of Glenn, was first in the room.

"Oh, my God..." he whispered.

Though Jenny didn't see a body, she knew Mrs. Hamilton was dead.

CHAPTER ELEVEN

IN THE BACK OF HER MIND she heard the waves crashing against the cliffs long before she roused herself from a restless sleep. It must be very early, as daylight just fringed the darkness. Turning over, away from the window, Jenny wondered why she had been anxious for morning. Then she realized she still had on her slacks and blouse from last night. The sound of a door closing jarred her sleepy uneasiness into awareness. Mrs. Hamilton was dead.

When they had broken into the virgin's bedroom last night, Martin had rushed to the tower area. The night breeze, damp and cool, blew in the broken window. A piece of Mrs. Hamilton's dress had caught on the window frame and trembled in the air.

"Oh, no!" Lone Willow's cry of anguish filled the room.

"Aunt Grace must have tripped, fallen against the pane." Martin's voice sounded hollow, almost unbelieving, as he stood staring out to the water below.

Each of them felt an emptiness, as though a part of them had gone through the window with Mrs. Hamilton, Jenny thought.

"I can't believe it." Martin sobbed and turned his face to the wall, his shoulders heaving.

"Poor Mrs. Hamilton." Lone Willow leaned against Bobby Black Bear.

Glenn was looking at the broken window and fingering the fabric on the frame. He turned abruptly and headed for the door. "Aunt Grace didn't just trip and tumble through the window," he said primly. "That glass and frame was shattered with force."

"Force? You mean she..." Martin's voice cracked. "Aunt Grace...suicide?"

The word "suicide" seemed to hover over the room like a foul-smelling smoke. Lone Willow gasped. "Oh, no. Not Mrs. Hamilton. She wouldn't. It has to have been an accident."

Jenny had only known Mrs. Hamilton a few days, but she couldn't believe that she would take her own life, either. "Glenn—" her voice sounded loud in the small, hushed room "—suicide is hard to believe. Just this afternoon Mrs. Hamilton was planning on discussing certain things with you and Martin. She was looking forward to it."

"Maybe she was shoved," Bobby Black Bear said, his face expressionless, his voice unemotional.

A tense silence greeted this remark. They looked at one another and then, as though afraid of what they'd see on one another's face, they looked away.

"Conjecture solves nothing," said Glenn finally. Of all of them, he seemed to have his emotions under firm control. "I'm going to the beach. Coming, Martin?" Glenn stood aside as they filed out of the room.

Martin blew his nose. "Yes. Be right with you."

"BB, why don't you and the girls go to the library. I'm sure we won't be long. It's too dark to search the waterfront unless by chance, the body has been washed ashore."

"Sure, Glenn." Bobby Black Bear led Lone Willow down the stairs to the library and Jenny followed.

WHEN GLENN AND MARTIN RETURNED, Jenny knew by their faces that Mrs. Hamilton's body had not been found.

"I'll call the sheriff. Alert him to the situation." Glenn headed for the phone in the hallway.

"Do we have to report the...the accident now?" Martin sat on the love seat, one hand on his forehead as though shading his eyes. "I mean, it seems so cut and dried, so...so businesslike. Maybe Aunt Grace is wandering around the island somewhere. Didn't fall through the window at all."

Glenn stood in the doorway, waiting for Martin to finish.

Martin looked up. "You know what I mean, Glenn."

Still Glenn didn't answer, but waited for Martin to go on.

"Well, hell, Glenn, it's just so final. Almost like we were anxious to prove she's dead."

"Well, then, what would you suggest?" Glenn walked slowly back into the room and stood just behind the yellow chair where Jenny was sitting. "Waiting until morning? The sheriff could have other business and not be able to come. This way we're giving him notice.''

Jumping up from the couch, Martin strode toward the telephone.

''I hate to mention this.'' Jenny felt like an outsider, but still thought it necessary to speak. ''Mrs. Hamilton called her lawyer, Mr. Williams. He was to come out Saturday. Shouldn't he be advised so he can alter his plans?''

''Why would Aunt Grace call him?'' Glenn asked in surprise. ''Her will's been made out for years.''

''Maybe Aunt Grace wanted to change it,'' Martin answered. He flipped through the phone directory.

''Did she?'' Glenn demanded roughly of Jenny.

''I don't know,'' she replied stiffly, bridling at his tone.

''You were her secretary. You saw all those papers. There must have been something. Think!'' he commanded.

''I am,'' Jenny snapped. ''And there was nothing. And please remember I was Mrs. Hamilton's secretary for less than a week. I know nothing.''

''Come on, Glenn, lighten up,'' Martin interjected.

''I'm sorry, Jenny.'' Glenn brushed the back of his hand across his eyes and shook his head. ''I'm upset. I didn't mean to yell at you.''

By the time the sheriff and the lawyer had been advised of the tragedy and Bobby Black Bear had gone to Mr. Alger's room to tell him, it was close to midnight. The sheriff and his men would come at first light to search for the body and the lawyer would be out before noon.

"I think we should all try to get some rest," Glenn said. "Tomorrow's going to be a rough one. BB, why don't you spend the night? I'm sure Lone Willow can fix you a comfortable bed on the couch. Matter of fact, you can use the small bedroom on the second floor if you wish."

"Thanks, Glenn, I would like to be on hand to help." Bobby Black Bear spoke in a firm but tender way. "I'll just bed down on the couch." His arm was around Lone Willow's shoulder. Tears ran down her cheeks.

"I'll get the bed linen." Lone Willow, her voice full and husky sounding, rose and headed for the second floor linen closet.

Bobby Black Bear laid his hand on Glenn's shoulder. "I am sorry, Glenn." He looked at Martin. "And this is hard for you, too, Martin. If there is anything I can do for you . . ."

Glenn shook his head, his mouth tight, and for the first time Jenny realized what an effort it was costing him to control his emotions. Martin on the other hand, had no such control. He held his hands over his face, sobbing. He had been right when he'd said that Glenn was tougher in times of emergency.

"Come, Jenny. I'll see you to your room." Glenn took her hand and with authority pulled her to her feet. "Try to get some rest, Martin. Good night, BB." When they reached her bedroom, Glenn, asked, "May I come in a moment?"

She nodded, not wishing to risk her voice. The events of last night and today had left her feeling decidedly weak. Nor did she want to be alone—not yet.

"Close the door, Jenny." Glenn walked over to the windows and stood there, staring down at the dark and mysterious lake. Speaking softly as if to himself, he said, "Aunt Grace was the only mother I knew. I loved her. She . . . she loved us like a parent but never let us forget our real mother." For the first time that evening there was a crack in his voice. Jenny knew the empty feeling he was experiencing. Until she had lost her parents, she had thought death of a loved one caused pain like a knife wound, but it didn't. It was worse than pain; it was emptiness.

Glenn cleared his throat. "I didn't always agree with her decisions, but I always knew she . . . she decided what she thought was fair and right."

Jenny walked over and stood beside him. "I liked her, too, Glenn. I'm so sorry."

Turning around, Glenn faced her. "And you, Jenny, dear," he said, his voice firmer now, "must leave here. Tomorrow. With the sheriff."

"No," she argued. "I can be of help here. I'll box up the papers and documents for the historical society. Mrs. Hamilton would have liked that. And I can help Lone Willow."

Glenn grabbed her shoulder, shaking her. "Don't you understand? You little fool! Your life is in danger. Back there in the library I yelled at you . . . to make the point that you knew nothing of Aunt Grace's business—for your protection. Don't you understand?'' He looked angry, but pulled her close, holding her tight.

She pulled away. "Life in danger?" she echoed in astonishment. "Don't you think you're being a little melodramatic, Glenn? There is no reason for anyone to harm me. I don't know anything. I was just the secretary, and for only a few days."

"Jenny, Aunt Grace didn't commit suicide. She wouldn't do that to Martin or me. She didn't accidentally trip and fall through that window, either." He hesitated, looking down at the floor and then back at her. His face was etched in pain and his voice held a note of anguish. "She was killed, Jenny. Then thrown through the window. To make it look like suicide. Or...an accident." He turned back to the window; his rigid back, like a slammed door, discouraged conversation. "I can't prove it yet, but I know I'm right," he whispered. "A gut feeling."

How could he make such statements with no more than a gut feeling? Her head reeled. She felt as if an evil, mysterious epidemic had spread throughout the household, twisting words, contorting thoughts, inverting innocent actions so that none of them were who they seemed to be—relatives and friends of Mrs. Hamilton. Glenn continued to stare out at the lake, as if it held the answer.

Putting her hand on his arm, she asked quietly. "Why, Glenn? Why do you think anyone would want to hurt me?"

"Why would anyone kill Aunt Grace?" Abruptly his pensive mood turned to angry frustration as he pounded his fist into his palm. "Because—" and his voice was hard "—because Aunt Grace found something in those papers or journal. Something that affects this land. And you must know what it is." His face darkened with the angry storm brewing within him and threatening her with its force.

"No. No, Glenn. I swear I don't." She ached to tell him everything, to share some of the burden of her knowledge, but it was the same old question. Who could she trust? Glenn had an interest in the disposition of the island, too. And where was he the night she was shoved down the ballroom steps?

"Well, what do you know, then," he demanded.

She felt trapped—wanting to tell and afraid to trust.

"Well, I'm waiting."

Jenny half laughed. "We found a recipe for mincemeat. Mrs. Hamilton was amused because it called for Four-Star Hennessey. . . ."

"Jenny, please." Glenn's voice was strained. "This is serious. Your life may depend on what you know."

"I'm trying to remember the various papers." Jenny hesitated a moment, then said, "There were several water rights documents. And some deeds. Lots of pictures. A tintype of the grandfathers. . . ." Her voice trailed off.

"Did you have a chance to look through Mother's diary?" Glenn asked.

"Merci's diary? No, Glenn. Mrs. Hamilton kept that with her at all times." The vision of Mrs. Hamilton tucking the land lease into Merci's diary appeared, unbidden, in her mind. Should she tell Glenn about Grandfather Clayborn's signing a twenty-five-year lease and that a renewal was not found?

"Well?" Glenn's voice was sharp, demanding.

"Stop bullying me, Glenn Larabie." But before she knew it, she was blurting out the story of finding the lease and Mrs. Hamilton's reaction to the discovery. Immediately she regretted her indiscretion. She felt as if she'd betrayed Mrs. Hamilton, and maybe herself.

Glenn blanched. Unless he was an exceptionally good actor, he'd known nothing about the document. In almost a whisper he asked, "Where is the lease now?"

She explained that Mrs. Hamilton had tucked it inside Merci's journal.

"I think that paper is important, Jenny. And could be why Aunt Grace was murdered. Now, with Aunt Grace gone, you're the only one who might have her information. Tomorrow you're leaving this island," he said firmly. "When this is all over, I'll come to Missoula to get you."

Before she could protest or, more importantly, question the "to get you," there was a knock on the door. Lone Willow called out, "Jenny, may I come in?"

Glenn strode to the door and opened it. "Come in. I'm just leaving. Everyone settled down for the night?"

"Yes. I fixed a bed for Bobby Black Bear in the library. I thought Jenny might be nervous about her room adjoining the . . . the other room. I was going to offer to stay with her."

"Thank you, Lone Willow. I'm all right. You're welcome to stay, but I'm not afraid." In fact, she was looking forward to being alone. She wanted no intrusions into her thoughts. Where would Mrs. Hamilton have hidden that journal?

"You could stay in my room, but my bed is a single." Lone Willow, her black hair braided, looked like a little girl in her pink printed robe. "I'll leave my door open, so call if you need anything."

NOW MORNING HAD COME and with it the sounds that had now awakened her fully. Doors opening and closing, motors putting, voices, subdued orders, hurried footsteps, all reflected the business of the day— the official search for Mrs. Hamilton's body.

Throwing back the afghan, Jenny walked to the window. Morning, like a shy bride, seemed to wait at night's doorway, hesitant of complete surrender to the day.

The air was chilly. She wrapped her arms around herself. The lake in the early morning light was gray and choppy, churning as if to rid itself of an unwanted body.

After bathing and changing her clothes, Jenny hurried downstairs to the dining room. Lone Willow sat at the table, her head bowed as though she were praying. At Jenny's entrance, she looked up, her face puffy from crying.

"Good morning, Lone Willow." Sitting next to her, she reached out and laid her hand on the young woman's arm. "Did you sleep at all?"

"Off and on. How about you?" Lone Willow reached in her pocket for a tissue.

"The same. Are they searching the beach now?" Jenny asked.

"Yes. The sheriff and his men brought grappling hooks and—" she blew her nose "—I can't believe it yet."

"Is Glenn down there?"

"Yes. Glenn, Martin, and Bobby Black Bear, too."

They sipped their coffee in silence, while a voice from the waterfront drifted up.

"Going to dive...dock...search among rocks...get hook...can't see nothing...water's cloudy...."

It wasn't ten minutes before they heard a shout. "Down here...scarf caught on rocks...cut it..." A few minutes later someone yelled, "Got her. Bringing her up."

Now it was quiet on the beach, a hushed funereal sound, no shouting voices, just a murmuring and then the order, "Get the stretcher over here."

A few minutes later Glenn led the sheriff, a large rotund man, and his two young assistants into the dining room. A grim-faced BB brought up the rear.

"Think these men could use some coffee, Lone Willow." Glenn stood behind Jenny's chair, his hand resting on her shoulder.

Lone Willow rose and left the room, returning quickly with a tray laden with cups and a pot of coffee. Martin came in, his face ashen, and sat at the end of the table.

"I'm sure sorry, Glenn and Martin." The sheriff gulped the coffee, a sigh of appreciation following his first swallow. "Terrible tragedy. I liked Grace Hamilton. A real lady." Holding his cup out for a refill, he said, "I'm going to send the body to the mainland. I'll want to talk with every person on the island."

"All right, Sheriff." Glenn set his cup down. "The library is available. Do you want us all at once or separately?"

"Separately." The sheriff shoved his chair under the table. "Might as well get started. Bobby Black Bear, I'll talk to you first and then the cook." Pointing at his two men, he said, "You guys secure the body on the boat, but don't leave for the mainland yet. Might have another passenger for you." His heavy-booted footsteps echoed down the hall. Jenny heard him ask Bobby Black Bear, "Why in the hell were her pockets sticky?" The library door closed on BB's reply.

"Sticky?" Lone Willow echoed the question. Her delicately arched eyebrows furrowed in puzzlement.

"Yes, sticky." Glenn sounded angry, but he walked to Lone Willow and put his arm around her shoulders. "Aunt Grace's pockets had a sticky feel. Murder. Someone murdered her." Glenn was pacing now around and around the dining table. Martin sat silently stirring his coffee.

Then they heard the sound of a motorboat approaching. Martin jumped up from the table and looked out the window. "That's Williams, the lawyer."

"Gad, he didn't waste any time getting here." Glenn's tone was bitter.

"Glenn, I'm sure Mr. Williams only wants to be of help to us," Martin said. "There is business to attend to in spite of our grief."

"You mean the reading of the will, dear brother?" Glenn asked contemptuously.

Shaking his head, Martin headed for the door. "I'll go meet him."

Jenny stood at the window, watching the boat dock. Turning, she said, "Glenn, I don't know whether it's the law or just the custom, but usually wills aren't read until after the funeral."

"I know that," he said, sighing wearily. "I'm sorry. I was just being a bastard, Jenny. Think I'll change before Mr. Williams gets up here."

GLENN HAD JUST RETURNED to the living room, clean in faded denims and sport shirt, when he and Jenny heard Lone Willow welcoming someone at the front door. A few minutes later she opened the living room door and stepped inside followed, to Jenny's dismay, by Keith Taylor. Mr. Williams and Martin brought up the rear.

"Jenny, my dear Jenny." Keith bounded toward her and hugged her tightly. Although she struggled to free herself, he managed to kiss her cheek and forehead.

Finally she pushed free of him. "Keith!" she exclaimed. "What the devil are you doing here?"

He reached out and pulled her close again.

"Let go of me, please," she pleaded in a low voice. The last thing she wanted was a scene, yet she didn't want Keith carrying on as if they had an understanding. She tried to squirm loose, but like a rope with a trick knot each squirm seemed to enfold her more intimately. Desperately she looked over at Glenn, but he had turned his back on them.

"Darling, when Frank Williams called about this terrible accident, I knew I had to come and bring you home."

"Please, Keith, let go of me." Now she did feel bad. Was it her fault that Keith didn't believe her?

With a sigh of regret Keith finally let her go. He shrugged and, with a rueful smile, said, "I thought it was worth another try...."

She looked around for Glenn. "Where's Glenn?" she asked.

Lone Willow shrugged. "Gone. Guess he didn't think he was needed."

Damn, she thought angrily. Why did Keith have to appear now.

Mr. Williams interrupted her thoughts. "Jenny. Jenny, dear. I am sorry you're involved in this tragedy. Little did I realize when I recommended you to Grace that I was placing you in an awkward position."

"Not awkward, Mr. Williams, sad. Mrs. Hamilton was a gracious lady. I feel honored to have known her even for a short time."

Glenn reappeared in the living room. Jenny tried to catch his eye, to speak across the room to him, but he ignored her.

"Thank you, Mr. Williams, for coming right out. We appreciate it." Martin motioned with his hand for Mr. Williams to sit down.

"It's a tragic accident. I'll miss Grace. Charming lady." Mr. Williams set his briefcase alongside the couch and sat down. "As I told you last night on the phone, there isn't much to do at this stage. I have the will your aunt wrote, which I will read at the appropriate time. Unless you need help with funeral arrangements?"

"No, Mr. Williams." Glenn spoke up. "Both Martin and I know what Aunt Grace wanted. A simple funeral. Private. After the sheriff releases the body, we'll go to the mainland and make arrangements."

The sheriff and BB stood in the doorway. "Glenn, Martin, I'd like to send Bobby Black Bear along with the body to the mainland. I've finished with him. That way I can talk with you and still get the autopsy underway. Save time."

Martin looked questioningly at Glenn.

"Fine, sheriff," replied Glenn. "Martin and I can go later to make final arrangements. BB, the Hanson-White Mortuary will take care of...Aunt Grace... when the autopsy is completed. And thanks."

"Well, then, Glenn, I can talk with you or Martin next."

"I'd appreciate it," Glenn said, "if you'd take Miss Fletcher, Aunt Grace's summer secretary, next. She'll be returning to Missoula."

"I will not," declared Jenny vehemently. "I'm staying and finishing my job."

"Now, Jenny, dear, Glenn is right. You look so tired. All this turmoil has been hard on you. When this tragedy is behind us, I hope you'll come back." Martin put his arm around her shoulders.

Pulling away, she turned to face him. "I wish you people would understand," she said angrily. "I've an obligation to finish the job for Mrs. Hamilton, to turn the documents and historical papers over to the historical society. And finish it I will." Jenny glared at Glenn as if daring him to argue. His glacial look sent shivers through her, but at that point she didn't care. She did feel a responsibility to fulfill Mrs. Hamilton's wishes.

The sheriff said, "Well, then, Glenn, let's you and me have a talk." He turned to Martin. "I'll see you next. You get your visiting done with the lawyer. Bobby Black Bear, anytime you're ready, you can leave for the mainland."

"When the sheriff is ready to leave, BB, he can take one of our boats, then you can bring it back. All right?" Glenn turned to the lawyer and shook hands. "Thanks for coming, Mr. Williams. We'll be in touch." Nodding in Keith's direction, he said, "Taylor," and followed the sheriff down the hall.

Lone Willow and Jenny stood at the window, watching the sheriff's men help BB into the boat so as not to disturb Mrs. Hamilton's shrouded body strapped to the bow. A few moments later one of the men shoved the boat away from the dock and leaped aboard. Bobby Black Bear looked up and waved.

Shortly thereafter, Jenny heard Mr. Williams saying goodbye to Martin. She and Lone Willow turned away from the window and said their goodbyes. At the doorway Keith stopped.

"Goodbye, Jenny," he said wistfully, "if you ever need me, you know where to look."

Impulsively she hurried to him and took his hands in hers. "Friends, Keith?"

"Always, Jenny." He gave her a crooked smile.

Hugging him, she kissed him on the cheek. "Bye. Good luck," she whispered. Perversely tears blurred her eyes, and she dabbed at them with her hankie.

"Why didn't you leave with your boyfriend, Jenny?" Glenn asked. "You don't belong here."

She started at the sound of his voice. "Oh, is the sheriff finished talking with you?" she queried inanely.

"Obviously," he retorted. "I was just in time to witness that tender scene. You're very convincing."

What was wrong with him all of a sudden, she wondered. If she didn't know better, she might have thought he was jealous. "For your information," she said stiffly, "Keith and I have been friends for years, and that was a final goodbye."

"If that was goodbye, I'd sure like to see your hello," he remarked sarcastically.

"Well, don't wait for it," she snapped.

"No," he returned slowly, "no, I won't." And with that he turned and walked away.

Exhausted, emotionally drained and close to tears, she curled up in the chair. What was it about that man, she wondered wearily, that always seemed to bring out the worst in her?

For a long time, she sat alone in the living room, her mind in a turmoil. But try as she might, she could think of no suitable answer.

CHAPTER TWELVE

IT WAS AFTER THREE when the sheriff finished with Martin, who emerged from the library visibly shaken. Whether it was the interview or the realization of Mrs. Hamilton's death setting in, Jenny didn't know. The sheriff had talked with the cook, Mr. Alger. With Glenn he had explored the house and the beach below. Now she, Martin, Glenn and the sheriff stood in the living room, making desultory conversation.

This, undoubtedly, had been the longest day of her life. Frequently she found herself holding her breath, then sighing deeply to make up for the loss of air. Thoughts chased through her head, pursued by the questions why and who. Why would anyone kill Mrs. Hamilton, and who? Why would anyone want to hurt her and who? Why did Glenn, and Martin, too, now, want her off the island? Who had made the noises she'd heard in Merci's study ever since her arrival? Why had there been a quill from Lone Willow's necklace on the steps leading to the ballroom? And why was she now hiding that quill among her sweaters in the dresser drawer? Did she think Lone Willow was involved? Why didn't she just ask her? Why?

"Miss Fletcher, I'll talk with you next." The sheriff's easygoing voice intruded on her mental questioning. He stepped aside for her to precede him down the hallway to the library.

Pointing for her to sit in the chair beside Mrs. Hamilton's desk, he sat down behind the desk and pulled a large lined tablet toward him. He flipped over a couple of scribbled pages to a blank one.

"Anything you want to mention first, Miss Fletcher?" He looked over the top of his horn-rimmed glasses, resting on the middle of his nose.

"No. I ... I just can't believe this is not a nightmare. I only met Mrs. Hamilton ..."

"Yes, yes, I know. Glenn told me." Again he peered over his spectacles, and his eyes, cold and glassy blue, narrowed. "He also said that you were pushed down the ballroom steps. Any idea who did that?"

"No. It was dark. I only saw a shadow—felt someone behind me." And found the quill from Lone Willow's necklace, she thought. But if she told the sheriff that, it would implicate Lone Willow. And she was sure Lone Willow wasn't capable of violence.

"Feel all right now?" the sheriff asked, and the warm concern in his voice belied the coldness in his eyes.

"I'm fine."

"Glenn seems to think his aunt was killed because she knew something—found something. The two of you were sorting old family papers. Right?"

She nodded. "And that's all they were, old deeds, water rights, pictures, correspondence." She didn't mention the lease or Merci's diary—both missing, and neither of them the sheriff's business.

"Was the shadow a man or a woman?" The sheriff shot out the question unexpectedly. The guilt over her concealments made her face burn. She bowed her head, hoping her face didn't show her embarrassment.

"It...it was too dark. I don't know," she stammered.

"Was there anything—anything happening at all— that was unusual or unexpected?"

Jenny remembered hearing Alger's words coming from the living room: "Money to make money. Don't be lily-livered now." But she hesitated telling the sheriff because of Glenn. While she didn't necessarily trust him completely, she didn't want to implicate him, either. Neither he nor Martin had had anything to do with their aunt's death. Of that she was positive.

"Well?" The sheriff had obviously noticed her hesitation.

She just wouldn't mention seeing Glenn in the hallway right after hearing Alger's voice coming from the living room, she decided quickly. While she recounted the scene, the sheriff jotted notes on the pad.

"You're sure it was Alger's voice, huh?" he asked.

"Yes."

"Thank you, Miss Fletcher. I'll check it out. Now when did you see Mrs. Hamilton last?"

"Yesterday, just about noon. We had finished sorting in the virgin's bedroom—Merci's study. Mrs.

Hamilton was going to have lunch in her room. Said she was tired. I went to the dining room for lunch."

"And that's the last time you saw her?"

Jenny nodded.

"Do you know of anyone else seeing her after that?"

She thought back a moment. Martin and Mr. Alger had gone to the mainland for groceries; Lone Willow was studying in her room; Glenn and she had walked to BB's. "No, as far as I know, Mrs. Hamilton was in her room alone."

"That's all for now, Miss Fletcher." The sheriff stood and walked her to the door. "And if I were you, I wouldn't trot down no dark halls alone. Understand?" He turned back to the library. "Send Lone Willow in next."

"All right."

"And Miss Fletcher, if there is any document or correspondence or anything else you think of that might explain this tragedy, you will let me know immediately."

"Yes, of course." She hurried down the hall toward the living room, relieved to have the interview finished and her acts of concealment unexposed. The door to the living room was closed, but she could hear Glenn's and Martin's voices raised in anger.

"Fly off the handle."

"Hell, yes. You're accusing Lone Willow of murder."

"Not murder, Glenn. If you would calm down, you'd realize that all I said was that Lone Willow was the only one in the house with Aunt Grace."

"And you pointed that out to the sheriff, I'm sure."

"All of this is academic, Glenn. Aunt Grace must have tripped and fallen through the window." Martin blew his nose. "She wouldn't take her own life."

In her mind Jenny could see Glenn's face darkening. The snarl in his voice was almost visible.

She knocked.

Glenn opened the door. "Come in, Jenny."

Martin, standing by the fireplace, smiled. "Poor Jenny, this has been difficult for you."

"I'm looking for Lone Willow. The sheriff wants to see her next."

"In her room," Glenn snapped. Immediately contrite, he added, "I'm sorry, Jenny. I didn't mean to bark. I'll get her for you. You look exhausted."

"That's all right. I'll just run up to her room." She turned and started for the stairs. She was tired—tired of wondering who and why. She was tired of the sparring between the two brothers. And the tension. She really was tired of that. If only she could find Merci's diary... whatever was in it had distressed Mrs. Hamilton and perhaps even accounted for her murder. Jenny hesitated at Lone Willow's door. Poor Lone Willow. She'd lost a dear and special friend.

Rapping on the door, she called out, "Lone Willow. It's Jenny. The sheriff would like to talk with you now."

The click of the lock sounded loud in the death-still hallway.

Lone Willow, framed in the doorway, looked small and helpless. "Oh, Jenny, I'm scared." She threw herself in Jenny's arms. Sobbing, her shoulders shook. "Evil. Something evil is stalking this place," she cried. "I feel the hatred, the loathing, slithering through the rooms like a . . . a snake." She trembled. "When Mrs. Hamilton was . . . was alive, her presence kept away such spirits."

Jenny felt encased in ice. Lone Willow had put into words her feelings about Lone Lake Lodge. From the moment she had stared into the dark lake and seen the giant boulders lying haphazardly beneath the water like city blocks from a ruined civilization, she had felt the uneasiness, the tension, the fear of the unknown. The rambling Lone Lake Lodge, filled with documents and papers and ghosts of the past, emphasized a departed era. But was there a restless spirit, dissatisfied with his time on earth, wandering the lodge, leaving behind a malediction for future generations?

She shuddered but tried to keep her voice from trembling as she patted Lone Willow's back and clucked soothing sounds. "Now, now. You're talking silly, Lone Willow. The sheriff is very polite and not an evil spirit." Her attempt at a laugh sounded hollow.

Lone Willow backed away. "It isn't the sheriff. You know that, Jenny. It's . . . someone. Someone really hates me. I feel it."

"Who? Glenn or Martin? Surely, not me." Jenny joked. But Lone Willow was a cold audience.

"Not Glenn. And not Martin, either, really. Oh, Jenny, I don't know who or why." Her dark eyes were wide and filled with fear.

"Hey, Lone Willow, stop it. We're scaring each other. Talk to the sheriff and then you and I will talk later. Okay?"

She walked Lone Willow to the library door and then, patting her shoulder, said, "I'll wait for you in the living room. It'll be all right. You'll see."

Martin was gone when she returned to the living room. Glenn sat in the easy chair, his legs stretched out and his eyes closed. Quietly Jenny picked up a magazine and sat down on the couch.

"How is Lone Willow?" Glenn asked.

"Oh, I thought you were asleep. Lone Willow is scared. Not of the sheriff." Jenny hesitated. It sounded ridiculous to say Lone Willow was afraid of an evil spirit. "But of something or someone. I don't know."

Glenn stood. "She has every right to be frightened. She's being set up to take the rap."

"It's not an...accident...not suicide?" Her wishful thinking dashed, Jenny's heart raced as fear pushed panic into her thoughts. Mrs. Hamilton was dead, but she had hoped it was a tragic accident not...she couldn't even say the word.

"Murder," Glenn said for her. "And if you had the sense God gave a goose, you'd get out of here. Now.

Whoever murdered Aunt Grace now believes you have the same information that she had.''

Her fear increased at Glenn's words. She wanted to go—to leave this troubled island and murder behind her—but still her stubbornness held her back. "Stop trying to get rid of me, Glenn Larabie. I was hired to do a job and do it I will.''

She thought of the quill tucked under her sweater. Should she tell Glenn? He believed in Lone Willow. He'd know what, if anything, she should do about it.

"Oh, Jenny. You fool! You precious fool!'' Glenn reached out and pulled her into his arms. "I don't want anything to happen to you. That's why I want you to leave the island. For your sake . . . and mine.''

They heard the heavy step of the sheriff coming down the hall and Glenn stepped back, leaving her breathless and confused.

The door opened and the big frame of the sheriff filled the doorway. "I got to take her in, Glenn." He sounded almost apologetic. "She's the only one with no alibi. So I got to take her in." He stepped aside and motioned to Lone Willow to sit on the couch.

She walked quickly to the couch, looking at neither Glenn nor Jenny, and sat down. Swiftly Jenny went to her and sat beside her. She clasped Lone Willow's icy hand. Limp and cold, it was as if it were dead.

"Miss Fletcher, pack up what Lone Willow needs. We'll be on our way.''

Jenny stood.

"Oh, and Miss Fletcher, I talked with Alger. You know, about that conversation you overheard. He was discussing the menu and the cost of food with Mrs. Hamilton.''

Jenny nodded but didn't believe a word of it. Mrs. Hamilton had been in her room at that time. Besides, she wouldn't have discussed menus or money with Alger. She would have had Lone Willow do it. But now was not the time to argue with the sheriff.

"Sheriff, I think you're making a mistake." Glenn took his arm. "Come. Sit down. Can't we talk about this? I'll get you a drink or coffee."

The sheriff remained where he was, standing in the doorway like a shadow, casting his suspicions.

"What about motive, sheriff?" Glenn asked. "All you've got is opportunity, and that's just luck—bad luck. Lone Willow happened to be in the house. How about motive? She... when Aunt Grace died, Lone Willow lost her benefactor."

"We'll check everything out, Glenn. Don't you worry about that. I'll want an inventory of Mrs. Hamilton's jewelry and valuables as soon as possible. I'll have a crew from the mainland out to check over Lone Willow's room." The sheriff looked over at Jenny, still standing at Lone Willow's side. "You—" he pointed his finger at Jenny "—skedaddle. Want to get going before the lake decides to turn rough."

Jenny leaned down and hugged Lone Willow. "Anything you particularly want, Lone Willow?"

She shook her head.

"Well, it seems flimsy to me to take Lone Willow in just because she happened to be in the house with nobody to give her an alibi.'' Glenn paced back and forth.

The sheriff moved aside for Jenny to pass through the door. ''That ain't the whole reason I'm taking her in,'' he said. He reached inside his jacket and pulled out a cellophane envelope. ''This here quill was caught in Mrs. Hamilton's sweater when we brung her up.'' He walked to the couch and fingered the quill necklace around Lone Willow's neck. The quills clacked mournfully. ''Not too many necklaces like this around anymore.''

CHAPTER THIRTEEN

EARLY MONDAY MORNING Jenny watched Glenn, Martin and Bobby Black Bear shove off from the dock. The scene, three men dressed in dark business suits in a speedboat meant for pleasure, was incongruous. Fog hugged the gray, choppy lake and the three men looked like dark shadows suspended in the ghostly air.

"Will friends of Mrs. Hamilton be coming back to the lodge?" Jenny asked, remembering the crowd after her parents' funeral.

"No, the funeral is private," Martin said. "Be just us, and Mr. Williams, of course. He'll return with us to read the will."

Glenn's face was drawn and his fingers tapped nervously on the edge of the boat. "Let's go."

"I'll have coffee ready for you," Jenny said. "Give my love to Lone Willow."

"Get Alger to fix some sandwiches or something, will you, Jenny?" Martin waved as BB, using an oar, shoved away from the dock.

Glenn looked at her and waved. "Be back as soon as possible, Jenny. Probably between two and three this afternoon. Aunt Grace's funeral won't be long, but it might take time to arrange bail for Lone Willow.'' His voice sounded loud in the funereal atmosphere.

''Have a safe trip.'' Jenny stood on the dock as the motor turned over and caught. Bobby Black Bear headed the boat toward the middle of the lake. She saw them for a few moments and then they disappeared behind a curtain of fog. Standing on the dock, she peered into the distance until she could no longer hear the motor. And then the deadly silence enveloped her. She felt as if she were the last survivor on earth and civilization lay strewn on the lake's bottom. Loneliness chilled her heart, her mind, her very soul. Maybe she should have listened to Glenn—gone back to Missoula until the mystery of Mrs. Hamilton's death was solved. But it was a matter of principle with her. She was not a quitter; she would finish the job. And, Jenny Fletcher, she thought, face up to it. You didn't really want to leave until all the pieces were put together.

Tucking her hands in the pockets of her coat, she walked from the dock toward the shore. The wake of the motorboat still lapped against the pilings. Fog accentuates noise, she thought. Even her tennis shoes sounded like boots on the wooden deck.

She started up the path. Trees and bushes were distorted by the varying degrees of fog. Sometimes a limb stuck out grotesquely like a dismembered arm and at other times the trees lined the pathway like spirit sentinels. The forest was deathly quiet.

She stopped halfway up the climb to catch her breath. Poor Mrs. Hamilton. What a dismal day for a funeral! There wasn't a patch of blue showing.

She climbed the front steps of the lodge. It was only nine o'clock and the day stretched endlessly ahead of her.

She had to do something to resolve the mystery of Mrs. Hamilton's death and free Lone Willow from blame. She racked her brain trying to remember a document, a bit of Mrs. Hamilton's conversation, a clipping, anything that would explain the tragedy. Nothing except Merci's diary with the lease tucked inside it. *I must know something,* Jenny thought, *something I don't know I know. Glenn obviously thinks I'm in danger.* Once she had made her position clear—that she was staying—Glenn hadn't continued the argument. Had he changed his mind about the possibility of danger? Maybe he felt that with everyone gone—Lone Willow, Bobby Black Bear, Martin—there was no danger. A sudden thought spun in her head, sending slivers of ice down her spine. Perhaps he was the one she should be worrying about and he had made other plans for her. No, that wasn't possible, surely. After all, she'd been with him the afternoon Mrs. Hamilton was killed. Unless, of course, he'd had an accomplice.

If I keep up this kind of thinking, she thought, *I'll be afraid of my own shadow.* Resolutely she concentrated on different items she'd filed for Mrs. Hamilton. The sheriff's words of caution, "don't trot down no dark hallways,'' flashed like a warning sign in her head.

The answer had to be in Merci's journal, which Mrs. Hamilton had guarded so zealously. Where was it now? Did she carry it with her in her plunge from the tower window? Surely there would be scraps of paper littering the beach then. No, it must still be in Merci's study, tucked away somewhere in one of the boxes.

She'd tell Mr. Alger about the refreshments and then scoot upstairs and search the little room again for the journal.

When she opened the kitchen door, loud music assaulted her ears. She hurried to the blaring radio and turned it down. Mr. Alger must be deaf, she thought, to say nothing of completely lacking in respect for the dead.

He was slumped over the kitchen table, head on his arms, snoring loudly. A half-empty bottle of bourbon sat on the table. Deaf? Drunk!

Apparently the sudden silence woke him. He raised his head and looked at her with one eye open. "Get out of here." His head flopped down.

She stood near the door, poised to flee if necessary. She didn't trust this man an inch. "Mr. Alger, I have a message for you."

"Mee-ish? What mess-ish?" With both hands he shoved himself up from the table and looked at her with squinted eyes.

"Glenn, Martin and Bobby Black Bear will be back from Mrs. Hamilton's funeral with the lawyer between two and three this afternoon. They would like some refreshments, nothing fancy, just something to snack on.''

He tried to get up from the chair, but flopped back down again. Rubbing his hand over his eyes and then his head, he looked at her. "How come you ain't at the funeral? Left you here to spy?"

"Of course not," she retorted. "Mrs. Hamilton's funeral is private. Only the immediate family and Bobby Black Bear and Lone Willow are attending."

"Let that squaw out, did they?" He lunged from the chair and teetered toward the sink. With one hand he held on to the sink and with the other threw cold water on his face, snorting and coughing. With his sleeve he wiped the water from his eyes.

"I don't know if Lone Willow was released to attend the funeral or not, Mr. Alger." She felt as if she were talking to a difficult child. She was afraid he'd throw a tantrum if she said the wrong thing. "I have some packing to do in my room. If there is anything I can do to help..." She backed toward the kitchen door.

" 'Anything I can do to help,' " he mimicked. "Get out of here, Miss Efficient Secretary. Get out!" he roared, brushing the bottle from the table.

She turned and walked from the kitchen. It took all her self-control to keep from running to her room and locking the door. As she hurried up the stairs, she heard him laughing as he slammed cupboards and banged pots and pans.

Once in her room, she hesitated about opening the door leading into Merci's study. Was she opening Pandora's box? Would Glenn appreciate her searching through family papers, more specifically his mother's papers, on her own? She stared at the door, her feet weighted with indecision. The lock had not been fixed since it had been broken the night Mrs. Hamilton disappeared. An ordinary kitchen butcher knife wedged in the casement and sticking out like a bar across the door held it secure. Glenn had insisted that the knife be used until the lock could be replaced. At the time, she had thought it ridiculous, since no one could get into the room except through her bedroom, and the door to that had a lock on it. Now she wondered if he hadn't had an ulterior motive. Perhaps he'd wanted to make sure no one entered the room but him.

She shuddered. What was wrong with her? She wasn't ordinarily a vacillating, vapory maiden. It must be the knife or that creepy Mr. Alger that made her jumpy. She looked around the room. She hadn't made her bed yet. First she'd straighten the bed and room. Then she'd tackle the boxes in Merci's study. As though she had only four minutes instead of four hours until Glenn and the others would return, she hustled about, making the bed, putting away last night's clothes. When she pulled out the drawer to put her sweater away, she remembered the quill. Digging down beneath the white sweater, she pulled it out. The words the sheriff had spoken repeated themselves in her mind: "If there is any document or correspondence or anything else you think might explain this tragedy, let me know immediately.''

Quickly she returned the quill to its hiding place and closed the drawer. What difference did the quill she found on the ballroom steps make now? The sheriff had found another one caught on Mrs. Hamilton's sweater. Swiftly she finished tidying her room. She'd find something in those boxes to prove Lone Willow was innocent and someone else guilty. And just maybe, Merci's journal might have slipped behind something in that room. Mrs. Hamilton had carried it with her from the moment she'd discovered it. Just maybe she dropped it or hid it before she fell to her death.

She jerked the knife from the casement and opened the door into the study. Merci's boxes were scattered about the room, with their contents in disarray where a search for the missing journal had been made. Determinedly she sat down in front of one and systematically began to go through the papers and clippings again. Once more she looked through snapshots of Merci, some with her sons and one enlarged print of her and George Lightfoot, Bobby Black Bear's father. On the back of the different photos were the date and names of the people in the picture.

Mrs. Hamilton had told her that after Merci's and George Lightfoot's drowning, she and Mr. Hamilton had come up here and quickly boxed everything. "I always thought, after time had eased some of the pain of her death, I'd sort through her things," Mrs.

Hamilton had said, "but her death hurts me still as if it were yesterday."

Jenny reached for the second box. There were more pictures, letters, old magazines, some sheet music, a marriage certificate and Glenn and Martin's birth certificates, a boat catalog and an old Sears-Roebuck wish book....

Suddenly she had the strangest feeling someone was watching her. She glanced over her shoulder at the broken window with the tarp closing out the lake breezes, and then at the door leading into her bedroom. Was someone in her bedroom? Alger was the only possibility. The knife lay on the floor beside the door. It might as well be lying on the dock for all the use it was to her. A shoe or a book, maybe? Quietly she got to her feet and edged toward the door. In her mind she planned to open the door suddenly and run screaming through the bedroom, down the stairs and out the front door.

She took a deep breath and jerked open the door, a scream already in her throat waiting to escape. There was no one. Limply she stood in the middle of the bedroom, her heart pounding. Then she heard it. Something or someone making a noise. It sounded like a door closing quietly and setting up a vibration, nothing loud or certain, just a feeling of a hushed, purposeful quietness.

Why, oh, why hadn't she gone to the mainland with Glenn, Martin and Bobby Black Bear? She could have waited at a café or done some shopping. But, no, she'd been stubborn, hoping to solve the mystery while they were gone. And now she was paying the price for that stubbornness.

She had to get out of this house. She walked back to the door leading into the study and picked up the knife. Closing the door, she wedged the knife between the casement and wall once more. Already she felt better, as if she had locked the "noise" in the virgin's bedroom.

The sun, she noticed, was finally beginning to shine, burning off the fog. Almost as if the fog had been her personal barometer, her spirits lifted. A walk to the dock would dispel her uneasiness. Maybe Glenn and the others would get away early. It was just a little past noon, but waiting on the dock would be better than waiting here.

She unlocked her bedroom door and stepped out into the dim hallway. She walked by the small bedroom, and the bathroom, and started by the door leading to the fourth floor ballroom. The door was partly open.

"Well, well. If it ain't the purty secretary with all the orders." Mr. Alger, obviously still drunk, was almost at the bottom of the ballroom stairs.

Jenny started to run, but didn't even reach the banister before he grabbed her. His hairy arms grasped her around her waist. He pulled her close. She felt his breath on her neck and the smell of stale booze nauseated her. "Let go of me!" she yelled.

"Not till you tell me what the old lady found." He shoved her against the hall wall and with his arm held her against it. With his other hand he squeezed her neck.

She twisted and turned, trying to get free. The man was a maniac. "Nothing," she choked. "I was just the hired secretary to Mrs. Hamilton."

Alger's hand tightened on her neck. Jenny could barely breathe. Her head felt light and her legs wobbly.

"Listen and listen good," hissed Alger. "I know you know something. Gracie always was a talker. But no one is going to do me out of my share."

Terrified, she struggled to make sense out of Alger's ravings. She knew that in some way Alger was somehow connected with the mystery. He had to be working with someone—someone within the family or close to the family. Knowing that Alger was going to crush out her life at any moment, Jenny tried to nod, to stall for time.

"Ready to talk, huh." Alger lessened the grip on her throat.

With a strength she didn't know she possessed, she brought her knee up and jammed it into Alger's belly. He fell back, and in that moment she took off down the stairs.

The sound of voices, shouting and laughing, came from outside. Surely Glenn and Martin hadn't changed their minds about guests. The funeral was private to begin with, and they certainly wouldn't be laughing and shouting. But she didn't care who it was. Even Frankenstein would be welcome now—provided he could stop that monster Alger.

She flung open the front door, Alger right behind her. There, on the front porch, stood four, hair-braided, blanket-wrapped Indians, now silent, expressionless and menacingly watchful.

CHAPTER FOURTEEN

FOR A MOMENT Jenny simply stood and stared, her mind a complete blank. But as the tallest Indian stepped forward and looked down at her, she forced herself to face reality once more.

What did they want? A handout? She glanced over her shoulder and at a better time might have burst out laughing. Alger, his puffy face frozen with fear, stood just behind the front door, making himself as flat against the wall as possible. With his legs spread out as though clinging to the wall and his hands wringing each other, he looked like a praying mantis and about the same color, too.

She turned back to the visitors on the front porch. "Good afternoon." Her voice, she noted subconsciously, seemed to have risen an octave or two. Whatever these Indians wanted, she realized, it certainly wasn't to kill her. Which was more than could be said for Alger. She gave a shudder, then looked up at her rescuers. "What...what do you want?" she stammered.

"I am Chief Hawk Who Soars. Our brothers have not received the boat permit payment from Martin Larabie. We have come to collect."

Before she could answer, Mr. Alger stepped out from behind her. "Martin Larabie ain't here," he snarled. "So shove off."

The chief seemed to grow before her eyes. And though she didn't see Mr. Alger crouching lower behind her, she felt his breath panting on her neck.

"A...sir...uh, Chief, Martin Larabie's aunt is being buried this morning on the mainland," Jenny explained weakly. He was a decidedly awe-inspiring figure.

Chief Hawk Who Soars bowed his head. "We did not know. Now Mrs. Hamilton is in the spirit world. But it is not she we want."

"That's what I'm trying to tell you. Martin Larabie isn't here. He won't be back until after the funeral." Jenny debated inviting them in. They certainly cowed Mr. Alger, but, then, she didn't feel exactly easy with them either. And what would she do with them for several hours?

Chief Hawk Who Soars spread out his arm to include his companions and then pointed down toward the lake. "My people and I will honor the death of Mrs. Hamilton. We will camp on *our* beach and mourn."

"You mean stay? Oh, dear. This really isn't an opportune time, Chief Hawk Who Soars. You see, the lawyer is coming back with Martin and Glenn to read the will. There will be business things to attend to and..." Chief Hawk Who Soars stood silently while she babbled. "And everything," she finished weakly.

"We do not intrude. We mourn. We wait." Nodding at her, he turned, and the other three followed him down the porch steps. At the bottom step he stopped. "Tell man who hides behind woman that we will be back for him. We know much about him." Walking single file, they stepped off the veranda and headed for the path to the beach.

Jenny thought about running after them, away from Mr. Alger. But before she had a chance, Alger reached over her shoulder, shoved the door closed and locked it. The next thing she knew he was running down the hall to his room. She heard his door slam and the lock click.

Knowing how terrified he was of the Indians gave her a feeling of bravado. She walked down the hall to his door and listened. Something thumped against it. She realized that Mr. Alger was sliding furniture around to barricade himself in the room. Stepping back from the door and ready to run, she called out, "Mr. Alger, what about the refreshments?"

"Git away. Git away from my door. Those savages will kill me."

Mumbled sobs came from his room and she gave up in disgust. The man was useless. She'd get the refreshments ready herself. At least he wouldn't bother her now.

She had just finished a batch of brownies and cleaned up the kitchen, when she heard the sound of the motorboat. It was after two, and could be Glenn and the others. Hurrying to Mr. Alger's room, she knocked on the door and called out, "I'm going to the dock to meet the boat, Mr. Alger. You'd better get the coffee ready.''

There was no answer. Probably sleeping it off, she thought. Fine defender he'd be if the Indians really attacked. She hurried down the winding path to the dock.

It was quite a welcoming committee. There she stood among four Indians. The boat loaded with Glenn, Martin, Bobby Black Bear and Lone Willow, plus the lawyer, Mr. Williams, roared past the dock and then, making an arc, curved in toward the pier. If she thought the boat scene in the morning had been incongruous, this scene was unbelievable. A tepee had been set up on the beach ten feet from water's edge. A fire burned in front of it. The smell of coffee mingled with the curling smoke from the driftwood.

She looked up at Chief Hawk Who Soars, thinking she ought to make polite conversation, but his expression of total disinterest curbed her nervous chattiness. Instead she waved at the approaching boat passengers.

Glenn was steering the boat and he waved back. His tie was off and his shirt unbuttoned at the neck. Martin's mouth was open in complete surprise. Then he turned and yelled something at Glenn, who shrugged in reply. Bobby Black Bear had his arm around Lone Willow. Mr. Williams might as well have been a statue. He held on to his hat with one hand and with the other clasped the side of the boat. The Indians could have been in war paint and dancing and Jenny didn't think

Mr. Williams would have let go of either. Boats were obviously not his favorite mode of transportation.

Bobby Black Bear was out of the boat first and helped Lone Willow step up to the dock. Jenny expected her to greet her Indian friends first, but instead she threw her arms around her.

"I'm so glad you're here, Jenny." Lone Willow hung on tight. "I don't think I could have come back—with Mrs. Hamilton gone—if you hadn't been here."

"I'm glad *you're* here," replied Jenny with a laugh. "I knew the sheriff wouldn't keep you."

Lone Willow stepped back. Jenny could see now that she had been crying. "Glenn posted bail for me," Lone Willow said softly. She walked over to Chief Hawk Who Soars, and taking his hand in hers, she looked up at him. "Mrs. Hamilton was a good friend to me. I loved her."

"Lone Willow, we did not come because of Mrs. Hamilton. We came to collect our boating permit fee from Martin Larabie. But we will wait in honor of the spirit world. We, too, lament."

"Oh, Bobby Black Bear, you remember Chief Hawk Who Soars?" Lone Willow turned and reached out for BB.

The men shook hands, but no pleasant words were exchanged.

Mr. Williams climbed out of the boat and stood quietly on the dock. Martin leaped to the wooden deck. "What's the meaning of this?" he demanded, walking over to the four Indians. "What do you want?" He looked around as though mentally figuring that his group outnumbered the Indian group.

Lone Willow put her arm through Jenny's and they walked a few steps away from the confrontation. Lawyer Williams followed them. BB held out his hand to Glenn, still in the boat.

"Martin Larabie, you have not kept your word. You have not forwarded your boat permit payment. But because of our respect for the dead, we will wait for the proper time to collect." Chief Hawk Who Soars folded his arms across his chest. "My brothers and I will camp on *our* beach. At sunset more of our people will come."

"Blackmail," Martin snapped. "This is blackmail. I have my lawyer here. He'll tell you what happens to black-mailers." He looked around for Mr. Williams. Seeing him heading up the path toward the house, he called out, "Wait, Mr. Williams. These...these Indians are breaking the law. I need your help."

"I'm an estate lawyer, Martin." Mr. Williams answered, not breaking his stride. "That's my specialty. Not Indian affairs."

"Come on, Martin. Calm down." Glenn laid his hand on Martin's shoulder. Then he turned to Chief Hawk Who Soars. "I'm Glenn Larabie, Martin's brother. I'm sure we can settle this." Martin broke into a run, passing those on the dock, and headed for the house.

"Your brother runs. We will give him a new name, Rabbit Runner." The other three Indians, nodding, smiled widely.

"You put up bail for Lone Willow?" Chief Hawk Who Soars asked.

"Yes. We love her like a sister, and besides, she's not guilty."

Chief Hawk Who Soars looked over at Lone Willow. "Two good reasons, Glenn Larabie."

"Listen, Chief, let me talk to my brother. He's upset right now. We just buried our aunt. The lawyer is here now to read the will. Then I'll talk to Martin and get back to you. All right?"

"We will wait, Glenn Larabie."

Lone Willow and Jenny stood at the end of the dock, waiting for BB and Glenn. Jenny was surprised at how happy she felt now that Glenn was back. She debated whether to tell him about Mr. Alger's drinking, his threatening her, then barricading himself in his room. But Glenn's face was drawn and he had dark circles under his eyes. Unpleasant news, she decided, could wait.

"You must have been frightened when Chief Hawk Who Soars and his mighty warriors appeared at the door," observed Glenn with an attempt at a grin.

"Jenny wouldn't be scared of any cigar store Indians, Glenn," Bobby Black Bear scoffed. His dislike of the chief had obviously not lessened over time.

"She should be," observed Lone Willow. "Chief Hawk Who Soars is no dummy and he's tough, too."

"Well, I was surprised...."

"I bet you were." Glenn took her hand and squeezed it reassuringly.

When they reached the house, he asked if she'd tell
Alger to bring the refreshments to the library. She
crossed her fingers, hoping the cook had sobered up
enough to fix coffee.

But she was out of luck, and was busy getting the
coffee ready herself when Glenn poked his head
around the kitchen door. "Where's Alger?" he asked.

"Maybe he's in his room," she answered.

"I'll get him." Lone Willow stood just behind
Glenn.

In a few minutes she was back. "He doesn't answer. Maybe he's sick or something."

Glenn hurried down the hallway, with Bobby Black
Bear, Lone Willow and Jenny tagging right behind
him. He rapped sharply and called out, but there was
no answer. He tried the door, but it was locked.

"I'll get the extra key, Glenn. I know where Mrs.
Hamilton kept it." Lone Willow headed toward the
library. In a few minutes she was back with the key.

Unlocking the door, Glenn turned the knob, but the
door refused to budge.

"I think Mr. Alger stacked some furniture against
the door. He was...upset by the arrival of the Indians," Jenny ventured.

With both Bobby Black Bear and Glenn pushing
and shoving, the door finally opened enough to allow
sideways passage. A dresser, chair and bookshelf had
been used to barricade the door. Of Mr. Alger there
was no sign. The window was open wide and the curtain pulled from its rod as though someone had been
in a hurry to get out.

"He's gone!" Jenny was stunned. She'd thought he'd been too afraid to leave his room.

"What went on here, Jenny?" Glenn asked sharply. "Did you have words with him or what?"

She told them about the arrival of the Indians and Alger's panic-stricken reaction. She omitted the part about his chasing her down the stairs and threatening her. It sounded so melodramatic, and now, surrounded by Glenn and Lone Willow and the others, Alger's actions suddenly didn't seem so threatening. "I've made brownies and it'll take only a minute to get the coffee ready. Lone Willow and I'll serve you, won't we?" Jenny glanced at her.

"Yes, Glenn. Don't worry. Get comfortable and get the business part of this day over. I'm sure Mr. Williams would like to get back to the mainland before dark. He mentioned that he had papers to file yet."

"There's no way Alger can get off the island, Glenn," BB said. "He'll show up sooner or later."

"To hell with him," Glenn grumbled. "Come on, BB. Mr. Williams said he wanted you and Lone Willow present for the reading of the will." He turned to Jenny. "And there's no reason you shouldn't sit with us. You probably know more about us than we know about ourselves."

She was both surprised and pleased by the invitation. "I'll get the refreshments and be right in," she replied.

When they were seated in the library, Mr. Williams cleared his throat, looked around the room at each of them and then began to read:

"I, Grace Litton Hamilton, being of sound mind, do hereby make the following bequests: To Lone Willow, my cherished friend, I leave five thousand dollars, in the hope she will complete her college education, and the cameo pin and my diamond earrings. To Bobby Black Bear I leave five thousand dollars and the diamond lapel watch that his father, George Lightfoot, gave to Merci, my sister. To my beloved nephews, Glenn and Martin Larabie, I bequeath the lodge on Lone Lake and the surrounding ten acres, the boats, the remaining jewelry of their mother's and my jewelry, all to be divided equally between the two. All stocks and bonds and any remaining moneys are to be shared and shared alike between Martin and Glenn. Lone Lake Island, with the exception of the lodge and the surrounding ten acres and Bobby Black Bear's ten acres, is to be given to the State of Montana."

Mr. Williams took off his spectacles and looked at each of them. "Any questions?"

"You bet there are, Williams," exploded Martin. Jumping up, he strode over to the desk and grabbed the will. "When is this dated anyhow?" Quickly glancing over it, he threw it back down on the desk. "Why, this will is out of date," he exclaimed. "Aunt Grace talked with me. She said she was changing her will. That's it. She wasn't herself these past few months." Martin turned to Glenn. "We'll contest the will, won't we?"

Glenn didn't answer. His hands gripped the arms of the chair, his knuckles white, his expression stoic.

"Grace did call me a few days ago," Mr. Williams ventured. "She said she wanted to make some changes in her will. She had written several of the items down and wanted me to incorporate them in the document. But—" Mr. Williams cleared his throat "—we all know she did not accomplish that."

"Well, Aunt Grace told me several times—just in the last few weeks—that the island was to be left as is . . . a family estate. There's probably another will somewhere," blustered Martin. "We, or at least I, will contest this present will. That's for sure. Aunt Grace must have been crazy not to have handled this. Diminished capacity or something." He headed for the tea cart and poured himself a drink. "Join me, anyone?"

"If there is nothing else, I'd like to get back to the mainland." Mr. Williams began stuffing his papers in his briefcase.

"Have some coffee before you leave, Mr. Williams." Glenn looked over at Jenny.

"Yes, I'll get it right away. And some brownies."

"Will you take Mr. Williams to the mainland, BB?" Glenn asked.

"Sure, Glenn." Bobby Black Bear looked at Lone Willow. "Want to take another ride?"

She nodded and followed Jenny into the kitchen. "You know, Lone Willow, I don't think Bobby Black Bear wants to leave you within calling distance of

Chief Hawk Who Soars.'' Jenny set cups and saucers and a plate of brownies on the tray.

Lone Willow shrugged. ''I think Chief Hawk Who Soars is only interested in one kind of an affair and that's Indian.'' She smiled, her eyes lighting up. ''But don't tell Bobby Black Bear that. I'm enjoying his extra attention.'' She picked up the percolator and they returned to the library.

Jenny began to think Mr. Williams would never finish his coffee and brownie. The room seemed charged with frustration, disappointment, anger. Absently Glenn stirred his coffee round and round. Bobby Black Bear, refusing any refreshments, didn't even look up when she passed the brownies to him. Martin smiled wanly at her. Poor Martin. It was a disappointment to have his environmental plans thwarted, but now Glenn's plans for the island were invalid, too. Only Mr. Williams sipped and nibbled, dabbing his mouth with a napkin after each small bite. Finally he said, ''Well, Glenn and Martin, ladies, if you'll excuse me, we'd better be going. I'll be in touch with you.''

After the three of them left in the boat for the mainland, Glenn suggested they take a walk. ''How about it, Martin? Join Jenny and me? It's been a long day. Some fresh air and exercise will do us all good.''

Martin slumped on the love seat. ''No, thanks. You go ahead. Think I'll read and get my mind off things.''

She followed Glenn down the path toward the dock. He didn't say anything, and she was quiet, too. She wondered if he was as disappointed in the will as much as Martin seemed to be. When they were almost at the beach where the Indians were camped, Glenn stopped. "I'm going to pay Martin's boating permit. After all, it's for the boat, not Martin. He just happened to get caught. It could have been me."

They stepped out of the forest onto the beach. Chief Hawk Who Soars had said more of his people would be coming, but Jenny hadn't realized he meant so many. There must have been twenty-five Indians sitting around several beach fires, talking and laughing.

After Glenn had paid the fine, they watched the Indians dance. With the flickering flames of the camp fires, the chanting, the drums, the dusk, Jenny felt as if she'd been transported back in time to earlier days.

On the way back to the house Glenn said, "Tomorrow, Jenny, you're leaving here. I want no argument. You are in danger."

She didn't argue, but thought tomorrow would take care of itself. The danger was over as far as she was concerned. Mr. Alger was gone. In her mind she ascribed everything unpleasant to him.

Nevertheless she locked her bedroom door that night and checked the "knife lock" on the study door. The sound of the drums from the Indian camp throbbed restlessly.

CHAPTER FIFTEEN

EVEN THOUGH JENNY was tired from the emotional day, sleep wouldn't come. She heard the clacking of porcupine quills and a door closing. Lone Willow was home from the mainland. She wondered if BB was staying all night again. She wondered where Mr. Alger was. She wondered about Glenn and how he was feeling. Most of all she wondered where Mrs. Hamilton had hidden Merci's journal. Now if she had the instincts of that snoopy secretary she'd replaced, she'd know where to look, Jenny thought. She tried to force her mind to think where it might be, but it leaped to images of Mrs. Hamilton, instead. Dear, gracious, loving Mrs. Hamilton. Who would want to kill such a woman? Memories of her funny little habits crowded Jenny's mind: the twisting a lock of her hair, her strict adherence to a schedule, her high heels, clacking along the hallway, her fondness for organically grown food, her desire to give the documents to the historical society. What a mess those papers had been in! Jenny was glad they had finished sorting and filing before Mrs. Hamilton died. That, at least, had made her happy. All except for the papers left in the funny file.

Abruptly Jenny sat up. The funny file! That's where the journal was. It was all she could do to keep from jumping out of bed that instant and running down to the library to check. She made herself wait until she knew everyone was in bed. Sitting on the edge of the bed waiting for the household to settle, she wondered if she should tell Glenn. It certainly would be reassuring to have him at her side as they looked. But, then, what if she was wrong—wrong about the journal's hiding place and . . . though she would never admit it aloud—her thoughts were not as selective—wrong about Glenn. The consequences of her misplaced trust could be disastrous. She pulled a blanket off the bed and wrapped herself in it. The chill both of thoughts and night enveloped her.

Midnight. Except for the creaking of the old house, she had heard no sounds for over thirty minutes. She unlocked her door. The noise as she turned the key sounded like a pistol shot in the silence. She waited. Everything remained silent. Turning the knob slowly, she stepped into the hall, and realized immediately that she had to have some kind of a light. She remembered the brass candle holder on the desk, went over to pick it up and lit the candle. Shielding the flame with one hand, she crept out into the hall again and down the stairs, carefully walking next to the wall, where the steps were less likely to squeak. At the second-floor landing she stopped and looked over the railing into the blackness below. What if Mr. Alger had returned and was waiting for her in the gloomy hall? Shuddering, she forced herself to go on.

Halfway down the stairs she heard someone cough. She couldn't tell where the sound came from. After a few seconds of dead quiet, she decided it had come either from Glenn's or Martin's second-floor room, not from the main floor. She continued down the stairs. When she got to the library, she closed the door and hurried to the file cabinet. The funny file, complete with rubber band holding its bulging sides, was there. She didn't wait to check to see if the journal was inside. She just wanted to get back upstairs and into her room before she was discovered.

Beads of perspiration were strung across her forehead. Her nightgown clung to her damp body. Locking her bedroom door, she blew out the candle and got into bed. With cold hands and chattering teeth, she snapped the rubber band off the file. Merci's journal was there.

Hesitantly she opened it to the first page, feeling guilty about reading another's diary. Tucked in between the first and second page was the lease agreement that Mr. Clayborn had signed. She set it aside and began to read. An hour later she knew why Mrs. Hamilton had been distressed. She could imagine the changes she would have made in her will had she lived. Merci's journal spanned her teenage years until her death in the lake accident ten years later. It was an event journal, rather than a daily one. She seemed to write when her emotions peaked in happiness, sadness or fear.

In the journal Merci told of her childhood love for George Lightfoot, Bobby Black Bear's father. During the Second World War George Lightfoot was in the service and listed as missing. Merci made a hasty and, as it turned out, foolish marriage to Anthony Larabie, a soldier she had met at the local dance. After the war was over, George Lightfoot returned from POW camp and married Mary Moon in the Face. Martin was born to Merci and Anthony and Bobby Black Bear was born to Mary Moon in the Face and George Lightfoot, but BB's mother died in childbirth. Laughing Star, Mary Moon's mother, moved into George Lightfoot's home to care for Bobby Black Bear. By this time, Merci had realized that Anthony had married her for her money. She moved baby Martin and herself into the virgin's bedroom, leaving Anthony in the parents' room. George Lightfoot and Merci started meeting again by means of the secret stairway.

Jenny lay back against the pillow. Secret stairway—she shouldn't be surprised. Lots of old houses had such passageways. The words from Merci's journal crowded her thoughts. "George was waiting in the cloakroom when I slid the panel aside," Jenny read. "I told him that I was pregnant with his child. He said, 'As always, you make me happy. You must ask for a divorce, Merci. Immediately. I want you with me forever.'"

A later entry stated: "I asked Anthony for a divorce tonight. He was very angry. Later I heard his boat leave the dock."

Eight months later Merci wrote: "George's and my son was born today. We named him Glenn. He has the blackest hair, but curly!"

Another entry: "This week has been wonderful. I have had George's son, Bobby Black Bear, here at the lodge for a visit. The three little boys play like puppies. Grace is enjoying them as much as I. What would I do without my dear sister and her husband? Soon George and I will marry."

The last entry read that Anthony had called that night from Risco. "It's been almost a year since I've heard from him. Why can't he leave us alone? He wants money. Threatened to kill us...."

At the end of the journal was an envelope addressed to Grace. It told that she, Merci, had hidden Grandpa Clayborn's agreement with Gray Wolf in the passageway under the third step. "The twenty-five years were up a long time ago, but George and I, after we're married, can re-lease the property to you and Bradford Hamilton."

Jenny was warm now and knew what she had to do to finish the job. She had to find that secret passageway in the cloakroom of the ballroom and follow it down to the third step to get the lease agreement. Once again she lit the candle. Quietly unlocking her door, she stepped into the black hallway. The door to the ballroom was ajar. She stood at the bottom step, looking up, reluctant to return to a scene that had caused her so much pain and fear. But all seemed quiet and it was something she had to do. She edged her way up the stairs. Once in the ballroom she headed for the cloakroom to search for the secret panel. The room was wainscoted in mahogany. Slowly she rubbed her hand over each ridge, pressing gently. *At this rate,* she thought, *I'll be here in the morning.* There must be an easier way to deduce where the secret panel was. She began knocking softly around the wall, listening for a hollow sound. Behind the door leading into the cloakroom she finally found it. Pushing, pressing and finally shoving inward, she discovered the secret passageway. A small landing with narrow steps led downward. Setting her candle on the landing, she went down the steps to check the third one. Nothing. Must be the third step from the bottom. She reached for the candle and hurried down. On the third one she lifted the step and, sure enough, found the box inside. Now she had to find the panel that opened into the virgin's bedroom. Again she shoved inward, and the panel opened just to the right of the marble fireplace. What an arrangement! Probably George Lightfoot climbed the fire escape to the ballroom and Merci came up through the secret passageway to meet him.

Jenny set the candle and the box on Merci's desk. Inside the box was the agreement and a copy of the lease, signed by Mr. Clayborn and Gray Wolf in 1887. There would have been another lease agreement signed in 1912, but according to a newspaper clipping, Gray Wolf died in a timber accident in 1911. Of course, the heir, George Lightfoot's father, probably didn't know of the lease, and Mr. Clayborn had simply assumed the ownership of the island then. Clayborn's obituary, dated 1934, was in the box. The write-up mentioned his ownership of Lone Lake Island.

She straightened from her reading position and walked about the small room. Dates and leases and deaths whirled around in her head. She walked over to the broken tower window. The night breeze ballooned the tarp, and the cold air blew in along the untacked edges. Shivering, she wished she had put on slippers, then realized that her cold feet felt as if they were standing on sand. The floor was gritty. Stooping, she wet her finger, touched the floor, then licked. Sugar. That's why Mrs. Hamilton's pockets had been sticky, she thought. Someone weighted her body with sugar and shoved her through the window and into the lake. Theoretically, when the sugar dissolved, the body would rise to the surface—except that Mrs. Hamilton's scarf had been caught on a rock.

She walked back to the desk and reexamined the lease agreement. The lease was not renewed in 1912 so...so Lone Lake Island, she knew now with stunning clarity, really belonged to Bobby Black Bear—and Glenn.

She felt like running to Glenn's room and waking him up with the news. Indeed, she was about to do just that, when she was suddenly aware of a presence. Was it someone in her bedroom or in the passageway? Before she could decide which, the panel opened and Mr. Alger stepped into the room. Under his arm was Merci's journal. Jenny had left it on her bed.

"I'll take that." He snatched the lease from the desk. "And now, Miss High and Mighty, you're through—not fired, but dead."

"How did you get that diary? I locked my bedroom door," Jenny whispered, terror almost robbing her of her voice.

"I've had a key to that room for a long time, Miss Efficient Secretary." He reached out to grab her. She stepped around the other side of the desk. She heard another sound coming from the passageway, and seconds later Martin stepped through the opening.

"Alger! Oh, my God."

Ignoring him, Alger lunged toward her again.

"Stop!" Martin yelled. "You've got the journal and the lease. The island is ours now. You don't need to hurt her."

"Fool!" Alger spat. "I've got a fool for a son. Don't you know we can't leave any witnesses?"

"Son?" Momentarily forgetting her fear, Jenny looked at Alger, then Martin in bewilderment.

For a moment Martin looked embarrassed, then his look turned defiant. "Well, you undoubtedly read my mother's journal and know most of it. So now you might as well know the rest. Mr. Alger is my father, Anthony Larabie."

"Grab that can of ether and the rag, Martin. I'll catch her and you knock her out with the ether. Then we'll shove her through the window."

Martin backed away. "I can't. I won't. That's murder."

"Where's your guts, boy. We're in the clear. Ready for all movie offers. Waited a long time for my rights and no one is going to stop me now."

"You'd kill?" To his credit, Martin was obviously horrified, backing toward the door leading into her bedroom.

"Already have once. One more won't make no difference."

Alger made a lunge and grabbed her. He reached for the ether. She screamed and kicked. He tried to put his hand over her mouth to shut her up, but she bit it and screamed again. He punched her in the jaw, knocking her down. Now she was being dragged toward the tower window. In the struggle to subdue her the tarp had been pulled loose. She heard the lake lapping beneath the room and the Indian drums beating from the beach below.

Now Alger held a rag near her nose. She smelled the sickly sweetness, heard his raspy voice tell Martin to help. She felt the night air. Still she tried to scream, but no sound came now. Martin's face seemed to float out of focus above her. She heard him crying, "No! No, don't do it."

The water seemed to be rising closer and closer. The air felt wet on her face. The last thing she remembered was a vision of the boulders, the miniature Atlantis below, and the destruction.

CHAPTER SIXTEEN

"WAKE UP, JENNY."

She heard Glenn's voice from a distance. She opened her mouth to ask why, and groaned in pain. Her jaw. Something was wrong with it.

"It's all right, dear Jenny. Not broken, just bruised."

"I think she's coming around, Glenn." That was Bobby Black Bear. What was he doing in her room?

"She must have gotten a good dose of that ether. She's been out for over four hours." So Lone Willow was in the room, too. Was Jenny perhaps dead, and the three of them had gathered around to mourn?

"Get another cold cloth, will you, Lone Willow."

"Cloth? No, don't. Please don't," she murmured, struggling to sit up. She didn't want to smell that sweet, sickening odor again. Hands held her back and she forced herself to open her eyes. She was in her room. In bed. A nightmare, surely.

"Welcome back, Jenny. You've been out of it for a long time." Glenn leaned over and kissed her forehead.

Last night's events suddenly stampeded through her mind. "Mr. Alger...Martin?" she questioned groggily, her throat dry and sore. "The journal. I found it."

"Don't talk now, Jenny," Glenn hushed her. "Just listen."

"I brought a cup of coffee and some juice." Lone Willow set the tray down. Gently pulling Jenny forward, she tucked a pillow behind her.

Jenny sipped the juice while Glenn talked.

"It was Alger, or rather Anthony Larabie, my mother's husband, who killed Aunt Grace. He also sabotaged the boat that killed my mother and George Lightfoot. I don't think Alger intended to kill Aunt Grace originally. She went to Merci's study that afternoon to look through her sister's things again. While she was there, Alger came down the secret staircase and surprised her."

"But I thought Mr. Alger went to town with Martin to buy groceries that day," objected Jenny.

"No, the night before, Alger had laid the law down to Martin about finding the lease and—"

"You mean Martin was the one Mr. Alger was talking to? I saw you in the hallway. I thought—" She stopped, embarrassed now of her suspicions.

Glenn shook his head, a wry smile on his face. "It was just a coincidence that when you looked over the railing I had just walked into the hall from the kitchen." He reached for her hand. "Well, anyway, Martin dropped Alger off just around the bend so he could double back to the house and look for the lease without being bothered. He was to meet Martin at four at the same bend and come back to the house with him. Alger appeared via the secret stairway in the virgin's bedroom. He probably wouldn't have killed her, except that he was so shocked to find her there he inadvertently called her 'Gracie.' Aunt Grace suddenly remembered who he reminded her of—an older, fatter Anthony Larabie. He hit her on the head and she was dead before he loaded her pockets with sugar and threw her through the tower window.''

"How horrible!" Jenny shuddered, then looked over at Lone Willow. "I knew you weren't guilty."

"I knew she wasn't, either," Bobby Black Bear said, "but it didn't look good finding one of her necklace's porcupine quills stuck in Mrs. Hamilton's sweater."

"George Lightfoot had given mother the same kind of necklace as Lone Willow has. Alger had that necklace and planted the quill in the sweater."

Jenny smiled. Someday she'd tell them about the quill she'd hidden among her sweaters. "Was it Mr. Alger who pushed me down the stairs?" she asked, remembering the smell of onions and the sight of onions drying at Bobby Black Bear's.

"Yes."

"But…but what about the smell of onions?" Jenny asked. She saw Glenn, Bobby Black Bear and Lone Willow exchange looks, obviously believing she was still confused from the ether. She explained how she'd smelled onions before being pushed down the ballroom steps.

Glenn laughed. "You probably got a whiff of Alger's apron—a real deli of smells."

"Alger certainly was no cook," Lone Willow said.

"No, but after Martin hired the snoopy secretary to find the missing documents and then Aunt Grace fired her, Alger—or Larabie—decided to find the documents himself. So Martin hired him on as cook," explained Glenn. "Poor Martin was hoodwinked by his father from the beginning." Glenn shook his head as though he still couldn't believe what he was saying. "Martin wanted the island for himself. Apparently Alger arrived at the school this spring and told Martin that Hollywood was willing to lease the island for motion pictures. The two of them could make a fortune. Only one hitch—the lease. Alger—Larabie, rather—knew this island belonged to BB's family and had only been leased to the Clayborns. Martin, knowing he'd do me out of an equal share of the island if he had the chance, expected I'd do the same to him. So he agreed to help his newfound father find the lease and other incriminating documents and destroy them. He didn't plan on murder, though."

"Who messed up the papers in the library, then?" Jenny asked.

"Alger," Glenn replied. "While everyone was eating lunch, he searched for the lease among the stacks of documents."

"Where are Martin and Mr. Alger now?" Jenny asked, her head beginning to clear. She was at least feeling more oriented.

"Chief Hawk Who Soars and his friends are guarding Alger until the sheriff arrives. Martin is in his room. I've contacted Mr. Williams about getting a good defense lawyer for Martin. He did keep Alger from throwing you from the tower window, you know.''

After Lone Willow and Bobby Black Bear left the room, Glenn sat on the edge of Jenny's bed. "You had a call this morning, Jenny.''

"From whom?''

"Your professor. He wanted to know how your research paper was coming.'' Glenn smiled, his dark eyes sparkling. "I told him it was just a matter of refining and typing.''

"Oh, no!'' Jenny laughed. "I've no thesis—maybe a book—but no thesis.''

"You stubborn little fool,'' said Glenn, half amused, half serious. "Why didn't you tell me what you knew or guessed. What if I hadn't been watching you?''

"Watching me?'' she queried, partly in surprise and partly because she had no intention of answering his question. How could she tell him she had once suspected him?

"The small bedroom just across from yours.''

"Was it you who coughed?'' she asked.

"Yes. I hoped it would frighten you and you'd return to your room.''

"I almost did, but I was determined to find that journal. You didn't trust me, did you?''

"Yes. I trusted you as far as your secretarial duties and obligations. But I didn't trust your judgment. You . . . you are so stubborn.''

"Persistent, sir,'' Jenny said.

"I stand corrected," he acknowledged with a grin. "Persistent and curious. I didn't want to hamper your curiosity, but I was still worried where it would lead you. So I followed you. Bobby Black Bear was keeping an eye on you, too. And a good thing he was. I almost didn't get to you in time. Couldn't find that damn panel in the passageway. BB rushed in through the connecting bedroom door."

"And now my work is done," Jenny said with a sigh, relieved it was all over, yet sorry that her job was now at an end. "I'll get ready to leave."

"Your work is just beginning. I'm a full-time job." Glenn hesitated, his dark eyes searching hers. "I'm part owner of the island with Bobby Black Bear, my half brother. I need you," he said softly. "Together we can develop this island for everyone to enjoy."

Jenny smiled, happiness at the boiling point within her. "I think Mrs. Hamilton would have liked that," she said.

"Will you marry me?" Glenn asked.

For a moment Jenny simply stared at him in stunned silence. Never in her wildest dreams had she imagined marriage to this most frustrating of men. Yet now that she thought about it, she suddenly realized that more than anything in the world, she wanted to share Glenn's life. Gazing deeply into the dark pools of his eyes, she replied simply, "Yes."

Glenn reached out for her. His hand touched her face, his fingers gently tracing her brow, her cheeks, lingering over the outline of her lips. Then he gently pulled her to him and kissed her. "Do you think," he asked in muffled tones, "that a week is too short a time in which to fall in love and marry?"

Jenny thought of her parents, their three-day courtship, and their marriage. "I think it's about four days too long," she replied.

**For the millions who can't read
Give the Gift of Literacy**

One out of five adults in North America
cannot read or write well enough
to fill out a job application
or understand the directions on a bottle of medicine.

**You can change all this by joining the fight
against illiteracy.**

For more information write to:
Contact, Box 81826, Lincoln, Neb. 68501
In the United States, call toll free: 800-228-3225

**The only degree you need
is a degree of caring**

Six exciting series for you every month... from Harlequin

Harlequin Romance·
The series that started it all

Tender, captivating and heartwarming...
love stories that sweep you off to faraway places
and delight you with the magic of love.

◆

Harlequin Presents·
Powerful contemporary love stories...as individual as the women who read them

The No. 1 romance series...
exciting love stories for you, the woman of today...
a rare blend of passion and dramatic realism.

◆

Harlequin Superromance®
It's more than romance... it's Harlequin Superromance

A sophisticated, contemporary romance-fiction
series, providing you with a longer,
more involving read...a richer mix of complex plots,
realism and adventure.